PERFECTLY MATCHED

D1545833

Visit us at www.boldstrokesbooks.com

By the Author

Share the Moon

The Marriage Masquerade

Gia's Gems

Perfectly Matched

Perfectly Matched

by

Toni Logan

2022

PERFECTLY MATCHED

© 2022 By Toni Logan. All Rights Reserved.

ISBN 13: 978-1-63679-120-3

This Trade Paperback Original Is Published By
Bold Strokes Books, Inc.
P.O. Box 249
Valley Falls, NY 12185

First Edition: August 2022

THIS IS A WORK OF FICTION. NAMES, CHARACTERS, PLACES, AND INCIDENTS ARE THE PRODUCT OF THE AUTHOR'S IMAGINATION OR ARE USED FICTITIOUSLY. ANY RESEMBLANCE TO ACTUAL PERSONS, LIVING OR DEAD, BUSINESS ESTABLISHMENTS, EVENTS, OR LOCALES IS ENTIRELY COINCIDENTAL.

THIS BOOK, OR PARTS THEREOF, MAY NOT BE REPRODUCED IN ANY FORM WITHOUT PERMISSION.

Credits
Editor: Barbara Ann Wright
Production Design: Susan Ramundo
Cover Design By Inkspiral Design

Acknowledgments

A heartfelt thank you to Rad, Sandy, Ruth, and the incredible team at Bold Strokes Books. I am honored and forever grateful to be a part of this amazing family. Thank you.

A very special shoutout to Barbara Ann Wright, editor extraordinaire, for your patience and guidance.

For my wonderful friends, I thank you for always being there for me. You guys keep me smiling. I love you.

And the biggest thank you goes to you, the reader, for taking a chance on this book. I hope you enjoy reading it as much as I enjoyed writing it.

CHAPTER ONE

Hannah grinned as she skillfully slid down the steep embankment as if effortlessly surfing a wave. When she hit level ground, she dug her toes into the mud and fought the urge to climb back up the hill and slide down again.

"Focus." She grunted as she nudged herself forward. Today was not the day to play in the forest, marvel at its beauty, or just sit on the ground under the dense canopy and listen to nature speak its many languages in a symphony of sound. She needed to move through the woods as fast as she could without pausing a single second to give her usual acknowledgments or pleasantries to all the souls who inhabited its space. Today, time was not a luxury she could afford.

A slight breeze snaked through the dense foliage, barely disturbing resting leaves as it blew past her body and tickled across her ears. To those who didn't listen, didn't tune their minds to the frequency of nature, the wind would have blown past as nothing more than a *whoosh*. But to Hannah, there were notes in the air, and they created a tune that carried a message. It was the song of nature, and she had been listening to it since she was a child.

She closed her eyes for a brief moment, stilled her mind, and listened to the information it carried on its wings. The cluster of twenty-two men and women behind her was rapidly closing the gap. She frowned. That was not the news she wanted to hear. She thanked the wind for the information, gripped the bow in her right hand a little tighter, and pumped her arms that much faster as she sprinted through the forest.

"Almost…there," she whispered around strained breaths. The pace she had maintained for the past hour was exhausting, and this obstacle course was the most difficult to date. But the clinking sound of her remaining arrow jostling in the quiver upon her back reminded her that one last challenge stood between her and victory.

She ducked under a branch and hurdled a fallen limb as she picked up her pace. When she saw the long arms of sunlight weaving through the foliage, she knew the forest was thinning. She would be entering the open field soon, where she had one last shot to seal her destiny for another year. She let the drumbeat of her pounding heart set the final cadence for her pace as she bolted through the last clump of bushes. She squinted in the stark contrast of the bright sun as she sprinted across the clearing to a pile of stones stacked ten high, marking the spot that could seal her victory for this year's competition.

"You've got this." She took a moment to glance around. Over her right shoulder, she confirmed that the remaining archers had not yet emerged from the woods, and over her left, she saw the silent crowd watching her every move with anticipation in their eyes. She nodded in their direction as she smiled. She had a comfortable lead, so what harm could there be if she took the moment and gave them a little show?

She catapulted into the air, and time slowed to almost a standstill as she reveled in the sensation of flight, those fleeting seconds when she cheated gravity, and the wind gave her a brief ride on its wings. She closed her eyes and delighted in traveling aboveground instead of on top of it. But as always, her airborne time was brief. Gravity swiftly reminded her that she was not designed for flight. And as it pulled her down like a scolding parent, she tucked into a ball. She hit the ground on her right shoulder, rolled once, and came to a stop in a half-kneeling position, her left leg bent forward. In a blink, she had the last arrow positioned on her bow. She pulled the string taut as she curled her index and middle fingers around the nocking point.

Hannah inhaled a deep breath and slowly exhaled. She blocked out everything except the tree—over a hundred yards out—with a white chalk circle on the bark. Somewhere in that circle was a green pea. She couldn't see the little legume but knew it was tacked dead center.

As she closed her eyes and let her breathing turn slow and shallow, she drifted into a meditative trance. She blocked the sound of the chirping birds, the sensation of the hot afternoon sun, and the trickle of sweat making its way down the side of her face. She stilled her mind. Talk to me, my friend, she thought, as the wind's whisper turned from the simple sound of a breeze to words that brushed past her ear and spoke: *Not yet.*

Hannah remained as still as a stone. She held the string taut and waited. She listened and obeyed, and in return, the wind never failed her. That was the agreement they had made. Her fellow archers said she had a *gift* and *talent* and an *uncanny instinct*. But nature was the puppeteer, and she was just the puppet.

Wait, the wind whispered again, and Hannah had to call upon the one quality she had never fully mastered: patience. Somewhere in the fog of her mind, she became keenly aware that the other archers had bolted through the forest and were closing on her. A slight twitch developed in her leg, a release of the anxiety that began to swirl in her stomach.

Patience, the wind's notes said in her ear; it knew her flaws well. Hannah stilled her leg, hoping her mind would follow. Victory would be hers if she obeyed.

Moments later, the slightest breeze blew around her, and in it was a single word: *Now.*

Hannah released the arrow into the capable hands of the wind. As it flew, she knew it would hit its mark and split the pea in two. She held her breath as a second of silence passed. Then two. Finally, the sound of the roaring crowd penetrated her mind, and the world around her came into focus. She slowly opened her eyes and blinked. She didn't have to look at the target to know.

Several other archers flanked her and quickly set their stance. Within a minute, several arrows pierced the tree. When a dozen landed within the white circle, the referee raised a red flag, signaling that the competition was complete. The positions for the island's twelve cupids were now filled. For the disappointed few who didn't make the cut, there would always be next year.

A flock of men and women descended on Hannah and the archers, pounding shoulders and backs as cheers of congratulations rose above the chatter. "Seriously, do you ever miss?" Piper said as she broke through the crowd and wrapped Hannah in a tight hug. "You do realize you're making the other archers look bad."

"What can I say? Oriana taught me well." Whenever anyone in public, especially her best friend, complimented her skills, Hannah always deflected the praise to the one who taught her the ways of a bow and arrow.

"Oriana may have made you a great archer, but we both know there are other things at play that make you the best cupid this island has ever seen," Piper said in a low voice. "I see the wind is still by your side."

"Always." Hannah smiled. "How else do you think I could—"

"Hannah." Oriana appeared out of the crowd, slapped a hand on her shoulder, and gave it a gentle squeeze.

Hannah turned and extended her arms, palms up. Oriana placed hers on top, the gold arm guards they both wore from wrists to elbows clanked together, but Oriana's bore the silver arrow inlay that designated her as the master archery teacher, while Hannah's had two stripes by the wrists, distinguishing her as a cupid. Most of the island's archers only wore a bracer on their bow arm, but those who could shoot equally well with either arm wore two. And Hannah and Oriana were the only ones, a distinguished honor that she was reminded of every time they performed their customary greeting.

"I see you have done well...again." Oriana's characteristically stern expression briefly morphed into a smile. She stood six feet tall, her long salt and pepper hair was braided with weathered leather ribbon, and her athletic body defied the evidence of age deeply etched into her face. But her most notable feature was a scar that ran diagonally from the corner of her right eye to the tip of her lip.

"Thanks to you." As a child, Hannah had relished any and all praise from her teacher. As an adult, that admiration she'd so desperately sought seemed misplaced. Her arrows, perfectly crafted by Piper, allowed the wind to easily carry them. Both deserved as much praise as she did.

Oriana snorted. "You have instincts beyond my teaching. But I hope I had a hand in showing you how to harness them." She had said many times that she knew where her teaching ended, and Hannah's uncanny gift took over.

Hannah felt her cheeks flush. How could she tell her teacher that the wind spoke to her and guided her arrows without diminishing the skilled training of such an admired instructor?

"A pupil is only as good as their teacher, and I was blessed with the best and most gifted master archer on this island."

Oriana threw her head back in laughter. "Always the charmer," she said as she patted her shoulder. "Always the charmer."

A hush fell upon the crowd as Nikita, Queen of Archer Island, approached on her dappled gray Andalusian stallion. She was accompanied by her lover, Anna, whose companion mare was creamy white. They were a stunning couple and well-loved and respected. Both wore full-length, ivory-colored dresses with mid-thigh slits that ran the length of the fabric, and both were draped in capes the color of a perfectly aged cabernet sauvignon. What distinguished Nikita as queen was the enormous, deep-green emerald ring on her right hand.

The crowd parted. Nikita dismounted and closed the short distance between them. "My dear, beautiful, Hannah. We honor you yet again."

Hannah bowed.

"Fellow archers and honored islanders," Nikita said as she turned in a circle. "On this beautiful day on Archer Island, it is my pleasure to once again honor Hannah." The crowd roared. "For the sixth year in a row!" Nikita held a hand toward Anna, who graced it with a golden arrow. "The cupid's arrow is once again yours, my dear. Well done." She placed it in Hannah's extended hands.

She bowed, took a step back, and raised it exuberantly over her head to more cheers. "Thank you, my friends and fellow competitors. I am humbled beyond words, and I accept this on your behalf." She motioned to the other archers. "You are truly the most amazing archers I have had the pleasure to work with and call friends. I'm honored to be in your presence." She placed her hand over her heart and bowed. "Now, please," she said as she stood, "everyone, join me in a celebration at Brea's."

The crowd once again exploded in cheers, then rapidly began dispersing toward town on horseback, on foot, or by teleporting.

As Hannah dropped the golden arrow in her quiver, Piper approached once more. "Shall I ride with you or meet you there?" she asked as she sat on the bare back of her palomino mare.

"Go join the festivities and order me a drink. Let Brea know I'll be there shortly."

"Sounds good." The slightest clicking sound sent her horse in the same direction as those before her, leaving Hannah alone in the field. She took a moment and glanced again at the tree that still held the arrows, but only one was dead center. From this distance, the pea was still impossible to see. She took a moment to lower her head and whisper her gratitude to the wind. Her words were answered by a small cyclone that circled for a moment before dancing down the field, picking up and redispersing debris in its wake. Hannah chuckled. "You are a bit of a trickster, my friend."

She whistled three short bursts, and within seconds, Bella, her black Friesian, was galloping toward her. The mare stood at sixteen hands, her lean and well-defined muscles flexing with each step that pounded the ground. There was nothing in this world more magnificent. Several yards out, Bella slowed to a trot, then came to a stop within inches. Bella lowered her head and nuzzled Hannah's chest.

Hannah leaned in and kissed her. "Hello, my beautiful friend, are you ready to get out of here?"

Bella bobbed her head and blew out a loud snort. "Well, all right, then, let's go." She grabbed a handful of mane and swung over the broad back. She took a second to settle close to Bella's withers, then bent to stroke her neck. Her earthy scent was as soothing as the smell of fresh-baked apple pie. She closed her eyes and inhaled. Bella was her rock, her Zen, her everything, and she'd come into Hannah's life in adolescence, when Oriana had told her that her distractions were getting the better of her discipline.

"Horses have a way of settling one's soul," Oriana had told her when she'd requested Hannah join her the night her mare was foaling. "The foal is yours. And if you two bond, you will share a connection unlike any you have yet to experience."

For the first three months, Hannah had slept in the stable with Bella and her dam, talking and imprinting as much as possible. By the time Bella was old enough to ride, Hannah had already taught her a variety of hand signals, whistles, and words. Now at ten, Bella seemed to understand everything about Hannah and vice versa.

And if ever there came a day when Bella wanted to leave, she could live amongst the wild horse herds that roamed the island. On Archer Island, it was against the law to force another soul into something against their will.

"Let's circle by the lake. How does that sound?"

Bella bobbed her head and galloped to the east as Hannah gripped with her thighs and curled her fingers tighter around Bella's mane.

"Run, my friend. Run!" It was another beautiful day, she'd just won her sixth cupid competition, and she was spending time with her beloved horse. She felt happy, blessed, and was living her destiny. She couldn't imagine a single thing in the universe that could ever compare.

Fifteen minutes later, Bella slowed to a walk. A crystal-clear lake sat at the base of a forty-foot waterfall, a double rainbow rising from the mist. Bella lowered her head to forage. Normally, Hannah would dismount, undress, and enjoy an invigorating swim or sit against one of the many trees and let her mind drift. But she needed to get to Brea's, where the celebration in her honor was sure to have begun. Still, she couldn't help but pause and take in the beauty of the area. This place not only grounded her; it spoke to her. And at this very spot, the wind had first introduced itself. She glanced at the tree that still bore the circle she'd etched into its bark as a child and let her mind drift back to how it all began:

It was the summer of her fifth year, and a handful of elders rounded her and Piper up with the other toddlers of equal age and began testing them on which skills were naturally inherent within them. They were placed in a large room filled with items and trinkets that represented every skillset on the island and encouraged to play with whatever sparked their interest. Hannah strolled around the room, letting her fingers glide over several objects. When she paused and displayed any sign of curiosity, she sensed the watchful elders taking notes and whispering among themselves. But as the day lingered, nothing seemed to hold her interest or entice her.

Piper, on the other hand, had been playing with a cauldron for hours, and while Hannah was curious about the artifact, it did not call to her. On her second rotation around the room, she noticed the tip of a bow that she had overlooked on her first pass sticking out from behind an anvil. As she slowly walked over, the bow seemed to glow, and the moment she reached for it, a tingle shot through her arm. She moved it from one hand to another as she mimicked shooting arrows. The bow felt so natural in her hands, it was as though it was an extension of her, and she somehow knew this was her calling. By the end of the day, when the elders rounded them up to return to their homes, they told Hannah she needed to leave the bow in the room. After her ear-piercing scream and full-blown temper tantum, they quickly agreed that it would be in everyone's best interests if she kept the bow.

On the morning of the winter solstice, Hannah and Piper were swept away to attend the Archer Island Academy to master their skills. Hannah was to study under Oriana, and since Piper had been drawn to craftsmanship and magic, she would study under Isabella, master fletcher and spellcaster. Hannah and Piper were called prodigies, and their teachers seemed to be in awe of their abilities.

One particular morning, in between lessons at the academy, Hannah went to the lake to practice shooting. She grabbed a stone, chose a tree, and etched a circled into its bark. She'd seen the annual competition of cupids recently, so she imagined herself as one and dug an indentation dead center to mimic the pea that had seemed to elude the skill of the island's archers. She walked off fifty-yards and marked the spot with a stone cairn. An ambitious range, but she was an archer prodigy. There was nothing she couldn't do.

She placed her foot next to the rocks, took a deep breath, and fired her entire quiver. But every arrow fell short. Though discouraged, she retrieved them, returned to the stones, and shot them again, one after the other.

By the end of the day, after hundreds of attempts, she'd hit the tree less than a dozen times, and none were anywhere close to the circle. The frustration wore away her patience and confidence. "One last quiver," she mumbled to herself. The sun was setting, and she needed to get back to the academy. She grabbed an arrow, nocked it, and took a deep breath. She closed one eye and focused on the circle with her other. The moment she released, a gust of wind swooped in and held the arrow in place for a few seconds before dropping it to the ground. She stood bewildered at what just happened. She glanced at the trees and lake. The leaves were as still as stones and the water as smooth as glass.

"Huh. That was weird." She grabbed another arrow and repeated the motion only to have the wind stop it and deposit it next to the other. A flash of anger boiled to the surface. For the past few years, she had been praised by teachers, showcased in exhibitions, and was being molded to be the island's best. She competed against archers twice her age, and now the wind had the audacity to mock her?

She remembered Piper talking about working with the elements of fire, water, earth and air, and how difficult and temperamental they could be. But Hannah was an archer, not a spellcaster, so why was the air messing with her?

This has to be a fluke, she convinced herself. With regained confidence, she rapidly fired the remaining arrows in her quiver. Seconds later, she growled in exasperation at the pile of arrows stacked a few yards from her feet. "Stop doing that!" In a huff, she kicked the ground, scooped up her arrows, shoved them in her quiver, and stomped back to the academy. Stupid wind.

When she told Piper about it over dinner, Piper said that, according to Isabella, the elements could be real tricksters at times. But those who befriended them would always have power on their side. "Either the air is having fun on your behalf, or it's trying to befriend you," Piper said. "If it happens again, take the time to pay attention because it may be trying to speak to you."

Hannah scoffed, certain that the wind was mocking her, and she had no desire to listen to whatever it had to say. Besides, what could she possibly gain from befriending the element of air?

The next morning, when she returned to the lake, she again stood next to the stones and nocked an arrow. If the wind decided to make its presence known, she was going to show it who was boss. She fired off the first arrow into stillness. Although it fell short by several feet, there was no interference. She grabbed another arrow, took a breath, and shot. A gust of wind swirled around her and slammed the arrow to her feet.

Hannah stabbed at the air in frustration. "Will you stop that!" She nocked another and pulled the string taut. But this time, she mimicked the act of releasing it while holding on to the shaft. "Ha," she called as the wind swirled around her. "Gotcha." She smirked as she held the arrow out. A gust of air blew dust in her face, sending her into a coughing fit. She threw the arrow down and shoved her hands onto her hips. "I don't know what's going on, but you had better stop messing with me!"

She grunted as a cyclone circled her. But instead of being assaulted with the sound of howling wind, she heard distinct musical notes within the whistles of the air.

"Fine." Hannah calmed her breath and her mind. Maybe the wind really was trying to tell her something. "If you have something to say, say it. I'm listening." The air accelerated, and Hannah became enchanted with a melody that sounded like the most beautiful pipe organ she had ever heard. It was a song, but she had no clue what the lyrics were. After the tune repeated a third time, she became impatient and stomped out of the cyclone.

"Go away and leave me alone," she grumbled. Whatever the wind was trying to tell her, she didn't have the time or patience to figure it out. She picked up her bow and arrow, turned to the tree, and shot. The wind swarmed on the arrow, playfully moved it around and guided it with forced precision into the tree. It hit the small divot she had etched in the middle of the circle.

Elated, Hannah jumped up and down. She did it! She not only hit the mark that would one day make her a cupid, but the arrow was perfectly placed. But her celebratory mood was short-lived as she thought about the wind. “Again,” she called. She set another arrow, waited until she heard the wind’s musical notes, then released. This time, the wind threw it against the tree with such force, it split her previous arrow in two. She grabbed the remaining arrows and fired them as fast as she could, one after the other. She stood in awe as each was carried with pristine accuracy to the tree, splitting the arrows before it. “Wow,” she whispered with admiration as she bowed her head. She still didn’t understand what the wind was trying to tell her, but that day changed her life forever. She shed her ego and made a friend.

By her late teens, she came to learn the lyrics of the wind and listened obediently when it sang to her. She still didn’t know why the element chose to befriend her over the other archers on the island. Maybe it had tried, but none would listen. Or maybe it saw something in her that the others didn’t possess. Whatever the reason, she was grateful.

Piper joined her from time to time at the lake. She listened and watched as Hannah shot arrows and relayed what the wind said about each one. Piper began crafting more aerodynamic arrows that worked better in the hands of the wind. She experimented with different feathers and materials for the fletching and a variety of designs for the point. Each one was tested and tweaked until Piper mastered the perfect arrow that could ride effortlessly on the wings of the wind.

By the time they hit their twenties, Hannah was the island’s youngest cupid, and as per tradition, she was allowed to choose which fletcher she wanted to partner with. *For Hannah, it was a no-brainer.*

And now, here she was, top archer six years in a row, with her best friend by her side.

She once again bowed her head and silently honored the wind. She might be the best archer, but she was still human, and without magic, she would be no different than the mortals outside the island.

"Mortals." She snorted as she raised her head and opened her eyes. The word was a bit of a misnomer. Those on Archer Island were as susceptible to death as everyone else. The difference was that those born in this land aged much slower, allowing them to live about five times longer than the average mortal.

The sound of laughter made her turn. She shaded her eyes and focused on two young women standing waist-deep in the water and playfully splashing on the other side of the falls. Hannah returned their waves and remembered flirtatiously splashing with a woman well-versed in the art of lovemaking. Her stomach flinched as she recalled how her body had responded under the experienced touch. How the sensation of lips and fingers gently stroking and entering her body had awakened such a hungry desire and had introduced her to a depth of passion she'd never known. She wondered if these women were lovers or if this was going to be the first time they would experience such pleasures.

Hannah smiled, shook off the thoughts, and took in the view of the falls one last time. "Well, Bella, what do you say we head to Brea's? I'm sure the gang is waiting for us."

Bella uprooted a huge chunk of grass as she began walking and continued chomping on the swaying clump until she successfully maneuvered it into her mouth. Once she did, she broke into a gallop, and Hannah's soul beamed with happiness.

Twenty minutes later, she slid off Bella and thanked her for her company. Bella bobbed her head and trotted over to Piper's palomino and the other small herd grazing in the empty field next to Brea's.

Hannah entered the tavern to another round of cheers and applause. This was her time to enjoy the spotlight, for next week, the bakers squared off and after that, the blacksmiths with their anvils and so on. The name of the island might have the word archer in it, but it held them in no higher esteem then the other inhabitants. Every craftsperson, artisan, and occupation was acknowledged and respected, and each held a competition to honor the best among them. And the first round of drinks after each contest came with a toast and well-wishes for the winner. Today, the tradition honored Hannah.

"About time you showed up. You missed your toast. We're already on our second round." Piper smiled as Hannah scooted next to her on a wooden bench.

"Bella and I swung by the lake."

"I figured as much." Piper slid a mug of beer in front of her.

Hannah cupped the mug and took a sip. The pale amber liquid was malty, with hints of floral essences. Just the way she liked it. On her many cupid journeys around the world, she had taken the time to walk among the mortals, sample their food and drink, and try to gain an understanding of their many tastes and customs. Most of the time, she found what they consumed interesting and full of unidentifiable, yet tantalizing flavors. As for their customs, most seemed a bit of a mystery, but all were intriguing. For the most part, she'd quickly come to the conclusion that mortals throughout the world overlapped with so many similarities, yet for the life of her, she didn't understand why they seemed to cling so tightly to their differences.

"Uh-oh, don't look now, but Brea is giving you the eye," Piper said in a low voice as she nudged her.

Hannah glanced at Brea, a curvy woman with long dark hair and a gentle smile. Although she was behind the counter filling several mugs, her eyes were trained on Hannah, and she raised a seductive brow, which relayed that she was in the mood for a quick hookup. Hannah raised her mug in acknowledgment but shook her head in a signal that now was not the time. Brea playfully pouted but nodded.

"Not now," Hannah whispered to Piper. "I still have my duties."

"Ah yes, the never-ending job of spreading love. But my question is, when are you going to find the same love you give to others?"

Hannah released a long sigh. Although she had shared herself with a handful of the island's women, she hadn't chosen to settle with any of them. And even though her body lusted after each one, her heart never followed. "I just haven't found the right woman yet."

"Maybe one of these days, I'll craft a set of arrows just for you and shoot them at you and a would-be lover."

"Don't you dare." Hannah wagged a finger. "Sadly, I don't think love is my destiny."

"You underestimate your heart."

"Maybe." But to find her true love, a few things had to fall into place. First, Danika, the elder reader of the night sky and the one entrusted to stare into the vastness every evening, had to see two paired names appear among the stars. She would then write the lovers' names down, and by first light, she would take her stack of parchment and divide the names among the fletchers. A special set of arrows was crafted for the paired souls and the tips dipped in a binding spell that bonded the two recipients upon a kiss. But if the two souls had not kissed within seventy-two hours of being shot, the spell would dissipate, and the magic would forever be lost.

Hannah had once asked why there was a three-day limit to the magic. Piper had shrugged and told her that was the way the spell had been crafted since the dawn of time, and no one had bothered to change the recipe. Besides, Piper had once said jokingly, if they hadn't kissed by then, the universe had obviously made a mistake.

Fortunately, the spell also had a magnetic component, and once one lover was in close proximity to the other, the laws of attraction took over, a kiss soon followed, and love took hold. That was the magic of a cupid's arrow.

"Well," Piper said as she wrapped an arm around Hannah. "If you won't let me craft a set of arrows for you, perhaps the magic of fairy tales will come your way."

Hannah chuckled. She had heard many charming myths of love at first sight, but she brushed off the stories as ludicrous and impossible. The destiny of love was found at the tip of her arrows; talk of anything else was just silly folklore.

"Anyway." Hannah downed her beer, then stood. "I should probably get going."

"You're not going anywhere without my arrows." Piper stood and slapped a hand on her back. "Come on, I've crafted enough to fill seven quivers."

"Seven?" Hannah whistled. "Love is definitely in the air."

"Yes, it is, and you need to tell the wind to blow some your way."

Hannah laughed as they waved a final good-bye to everyone and headed to Piper's workshop. She had wondered from time to time what love felt like. Was it a deeper form of the lust she had come to know, or did it truly hold a magic all its own? She shrugged. She would probably never have an answer, and for the first time, that thought unnerved her. She was the deliverer of an emotion that had inspired the most magnificent forms of artistic expression and could make people do the most altruistic things toward other souls. Yet, the other side of that same emotion could bring forth an incredible expression of hate and destruction. Hannah had always been in awe of how one emotion could elicit such powerful responses, and she wondered again if she would ever experience its influence.

❖

Hannah sat with her feet dangling over the rooftop of a bakery across the street from a TV station in Las Vegas, and her stomach grumbled as the smell of freshly baked pastries filled the air. The excitement of the afternoon's events coupled with a long day of matchmaking were catching up with her, and fatigue and hunger were settling in. Maybe, she thought as she pulled the remaining two arrows out of her quiver and carefully untied the twine wrapped around them, she would swing by Brea's place after she finished and pick up a nice meal. Or maybe, she wondered as she watched the red Mercedes sports car speed into the parking lot and come to an abrupt screeching halt, she could talk Brea into bringing some food over for a relaxing evening at her place. She smiled at the thought as arrow number one was set and nocked in a matter of seconds.

She was invisible to all mortals while performing her duties, so she didn't worry about being seen as she swung her legs back and forth and let the heels of her sandals thump against the wall. She aimed at the car, and the moment the woman stepped out, Hannah's arrow pierced and vaporized in her heart. Thanks to Piper's skilled craftmanship, her targets never felt a thing, not even the slightest pinprick. But they did always pause and shiver, a reaction to Piper's binding spell releasing in their body.

"One down," she whispered to herself as she nocked the remaining arrow and waited for mark number two to emerge from the building. This was going to be an easy one-two shot. Coworker wannabe lovebirds always were. The woman from the Mercedes hustled across the parking lot toward the door, and as if on cue, the second mark pushed it open. Hannah watched them have a brief exchange in the doorway as she waited for a clean shot. "Come on," she whispered. "Move just a bit more to the—"

But the moment the second mark stepped out from behind the door, she glanced right at Hannah. Her breath caught as she stared into the most amazing dark-emerald eyes she had ever seen. They were the color of Nikita's ring, and at the exact second that the wind whispered in her ear to release the arrow, she was listening to whispers of another kind, and they were tingling their way up her body. By the time she realized her momentary distraction, she shrugged off the unexpected emotion, then sent the arrow flying. But a strange gust of wind blew the arrow to the left. Hannah sat in stunned disbelief as it evaporated into the side of the building.

"Oh sh—" Hannah couldn't even complete the word as she was whisked off the rooftop and teleported back to the island.

CHAPTER TWO

Payson Martin squinted at the roof of the bakery across the street from the station. A reflection caught her eye and made her gasp. She could have sworn she'd seen a woman sitting on the roof, dangling her legs while pointing a bow and arrow at her. When their eyes had met, Payson had felt a surge of heat rush through her, coupled with an odd sensation, as though they were somehow connected. But a blink later, the image of the woman was gone.

Payson shook her head and thought again about how sleep-deprived she had been lately. "You're hallucinating about gorgeous women. You really do need a vacation," she mumbled as she shuffled across the street and followed the smell of deliciousness into the bakery.

"Hey, Payson," Sam said as his arm feebly rose in a shaky wave.

"Hi, Sam, how are you doing today?" Two years ago, when his wife of fifty-five years and the baker behind their business had died, Payson had made it a habit to buy a bag of pastries from him every day. She'd worried his business would suffer, but fortunately, Sam's daughter, Amanda, had stepped in, and she was every bit as good—if not better—of a pastry chef.

"Can't complain. I'm upright and breathing, so there's that."

Payson chuckled as she approached the counter. "Well, then, I'd say it's a good day."

"What can I get you?" He grabbed a bag and pulled out two sheets of pastry paper.

She lingered as though scrutinizing every item because she knew Sam would take advantage of the time and fill her in on a story or two about his wife.

"Did I ever tell you," he asked, "about the time Dottie and I…" And off to memory lane he went. Today, Payson was whisked away to a small village in Tuscany on an anniversary vacation he and his wife had taken forty years ago. As she listened, she pointed to several pastries and held up fingers to let him know how many of each so she didn't interrupt his story. When they meandered to the end of the counter, her mind was already drifting back to the many phone calls she needed to return and scripts yet to be written before the night's newscast.

Sam seemed to sense this and always timed his stories to coincide. This was their dance, and Payson made it a point to give him the one thing in life he seemed to be needing the most…companionship. Or maybe that was more a reflection of her. She had seen the faraway stare of loneliness cloud his tear-stained eyes more than once, and she knew what that felt like. Sam seemed to spend as much time at the bakery as she did at the station, and maybe that was because both dreaded going home to a recently empty void that was once filled with happiness.

She made a mental note: when things slowed down at work, she would take him out to dinner. Maybe even make it a weekly ritual. It would be good for both of them.

As she left the store and crossed the street back to the station, a gut feeling told her to turn and glance again at the roof. A twinge of hope shot though her as the image of the woman with short black hair, light brown skin, muscular arms, and a gladiator costume reappeared in her mind. "I know you were there," she whispered as she stared at the vacant roof. As if saying it out loud would bring the mysterious woman back. But after a moment, she lowered her head and sighed. Yeah, she grumbled as she approached the backdoor, she really did need a vacation.

She swiped the badge that hung from a lanyard around her neck and after hearing the familiar beep, entered the building. She was instantly hit with a barrage of sounds and a flurry of activity. She smiled and nodded to several people as she meandered into the open newsroom stuffed with clusters of low-panel cubicles, some vacant, others occupied. She tossed the bag of pastries on her desk and flopped in her chair. She exhaled a long sigh of exhaustion as she fired up her computer. She had been working five solid weeks without a day off, and the stress was beginning to take its toll.

"Hey." Her best friend Tegan hiked herself on top of the desk and grabbed the bag.

"Have you heard about anything being staged across the street on the roof of Sam's bakery?" Payson asked as she logged in to her computer.

Tegan pulled out a scone. "What, like a publicity stunt or something?"

"Yeah, something that involves a gorgeous woman and a bow and arrow?"

"No. I haven't heard of anything, but it sounds sexy. Was she scantily clad?"

"No, she didn't look like one of the club girls. She was wearing some sort of sexy Roman costume, with sandals that laced up her legs. More like a Caesar's Palace kind of outfit, but a little different. Her clothing was more authentic-looking, not quite so campy. Oh, and she was really muscular, like she definitely hits the gym."

"Hmm." Tegan shrugged. "Sounds intriguing. If I hear of anything, I'll let you know."

"Thanks." Payson grabbed a muffin, pulled the top off, and discarded the rest.

"Oh hey," Tegan mumbled in between chewing, "I was talking to my friend at the Mirage, and I can get us tickets for Saturday night to see—"

Payson shook her head as she interrupted. "I'm working all weekend."

"Again?"

She nodded.

"You, my friend, need a life," Tegan said as she brushed a few rogue crumbs off her shirt.

"I have a life," Payson mumbled.

Tegan waved a scolding finger. "No, you don't…you have work. And work is not a life."

"True, but work pays the bills."

"A lot of things can pay the bills. At least tell me you put in for time off."

"I did."

"And?"

"And it was turned down. Jason said that until they can hire another producer, I need to be here." She glanced at the glass corner office and the overweight balding man leaning back so far in his chair, it looked like it was about to snap. He was taking sips of coffee during what appeared to be a very animated phone call.

"Screw Jason. That's bullshit, and you know it." Tegan pointed to the brochure of the exclusive, all-woman tropical island retreat that was tacked to Payson's cubicle wall. "Thought you already put money down."

"I did. They said they would refund my deposit, but I told them to hold on to it. I still plan on getting there someday."

She choked down the bitter taste of those words. After years of financial struggles, she had finally scraped enough money together to take a vacation. She'd put in for her time off four months ago, and Jason had approved it with the stipulation that Ryan, the weekend news producer, agreed to cover her shift.

He did, so she got online, booked her reservation, and sealed it with a deposit. She was finally going on a much-needed vacation. She had already bought new clothes and visualized days of soaking up the sun, drinking alcohol-laced multi-colored beverages, and maybe even meeting someone special. She was going to get away from the newsworthy horrors of humanity and unplug her life for ten glorious days.

She sighed now as she looked at the brochure of a woman smiling with a tropical drink in hand under a waterfall. She could almost hear the water cascading around her and smell the salt air mixed with her coconut sunscreen.

"Payson!" Jason's raspy voice raced across the newsroom and jolted her back from paradise. "My office, now."

Tegan bent and looked her in the eyes. "Honey, I'm saying this as your best friend, you need to get out of this job and get a life before this place completely drains your soul."

"Too late for that." Payson gathered her notebook and handed Tegan a piece of paper as she shuffled out of her cubicle. "I need you to check on this. If it pans out, you'll go live for your first hit at seven after the hour."

"Someone's driving a tank down the north end of the strip?" She looked up. "Is this for real?"

"Don't know, that's why I want you to make some calls and see if it checks out."

"Why can't normal things ever happen in this city?" Tegan grumbled as she grabbed a second scone and hopped off the desk.

"Because this city wouldn't know what to do with normal," Payson said over her shoulder as she shyly approached Jason's office with a light knuckle tap to his open glass door. He was the news director, and he lived and breathed all things news. He was in his office first thing in the morning and didn't leave until late at night. He was in a perpetual bad mood, and every breathing soul that crossed his path seemed to annoy him. Payson's shoulders slumped as she saw a reflection of herself twenty years from now if she continued down the same road. "Hey, Jason, you wanted to see me?"

He gestured to two chairs at the opposite end of his desk. Payson slid into one. "I just got off the phone with someone from corporate, and something odd came up. Apparently, they're sending someone to shadow you for a few days and help you out a bit."

"Wait, what? I'm getting a temp? I thought you said—"

"I know what I said, and that still stands. No new hires and no temps." He glared at her over his reading glasses.

"So back up. If there's no new hires and no temps, then why am I getting help?"

He tore a strip of paper from his notebook and flicked it across his desk. "Because this one's coming from corporate, so it's not costing me anything."

She gently picked up the paper and scanned it. In a scribble that could rival a toddler's were three barely recognizable words: *Corporate. Temp. Payson.* She turned the paper over to see if there was more information that would give her a clue as to what this was all about, but there wasn't. She frowned. While she could use the help, having someone tripping over her was not what she needed. Producing was a fast-paced, stressful job; having someone hover over her shoulder asking a barrage of questions while she was trying to work was going to frustrate the hell out of her. "Why me?"

"Thought you needed help?"

"I do, as in, a seasoned full-time producer with years of knowledge under their belt so I can go on vacation, kind of help."

He tossed his reading glasses on the desk and wagged a finger at her. "We're not talking about your vacation again. That topic was already put to bed."

"I need a break, Jason," she pleaded as she slumped in her chair.

"You'll get one…eventually. And don't get mad at me. Ryan's the one who left with only a week's notice."

She remembered the day Ryan came in and announced that he was jumping ship for a marketing position at one of the casinos. He'd apologized for the bind that would cause her but had said it was an opportunity he just couldn't pass up. And as he'd rambled on about the new position, she'd watched his lips move without comprehending any of the words because her head was pounding with the reality of the ripple effect his leaving would have on her vacation. "Have you even started the interview process for that position yet?"

"What about the statement, no new hires, don't you understand?" he snapped.

"I'm burned-out, Jason. We need another producer."

"And you think I don't know that?" He grumbled as he leaned over and referenced a folder sitting on his desk. "I have a broken studio camera, our news desk is in desperate need of an upgrade, and the satellite vans need to be wrapped with our new logo. Last week, I sent the proposed budget in for next year, and some bean pusher at corporate wrung it out like a wet rag. The station is hemorrhaging money, and if we don't get our ad revenue up, there may be another round of layoffs." He glared at her as he settled back in his chair. "So which of those do you think I should sacrifice so I can hire someone to fill the producer position so you can take your little vacation?"

"That's not fair," she bit back.

"Look." He pinched the bridge of his nose and let out a sigh. "You'll get your vacation, but for right now, just work with me while I figure out how to move the numbers around. Okay?"

Payson reluctantly nodded as she glanced again at the paper. "Seriously, what's this temp thing really about?"

"You're holding everything I know," he muttered. "They said something about an experimental program they were trying where they send temps out on a rotating basis to some of the stations to help offset some costs. Truthfully, they were a little light on the details, and I didn't pepper them with questions because frankly, I really don't give a damn who they send to follow you around, as long as it doesn't come out of my budget." He folded his arms. "You and I both know that when it comes to this station, corporate can make some pretty dumbass decisions. They're a flock of idiots, as far as I'm concerned, and you didn't hear that from me. Anyway…" He waved dismissively. "That's the way it is for now, so I'm asking you to just deal with it, okay?"

"What choice do I have?"

"None. Until corporate figures out what to do with this station, things aren't gonna be pretty around here."

Last year, their station had been swallowed up in an acquisition by a mega corporation that had their eye on a profitable chain of appliance stores in the western region. The fact that a handful of small TV stations was also in that portfolio seemed to be of little concern to them. Rumors started flying about their new parent company either shutting down or selling off the stations. Broadcast news had been struggling for years, and everyone knew the view on the horizon wasn't bright. This wasn't a storm that was going to blow over; this was a reflection of the times, and the advertising dollars that had once netted them millions were being spent elsewhere.

"Why don't you give the temp to someone else? Jerry in engineering is swamped."

"Because they specifically said she's your temp, so congratulations, you get to play babysitter for the next few days. End of discussion."

"Great."

"Oh, don't look so down. There are worse things in the world. Just look at today's national news."

True. Compared to what was going on in the world, there were plenty of worse things, but in Payson's little space on this planet right here and now, this news was definitely not welcoming. "When does the temp start?"

"Immediately."

"What? They start today? But—"

He held up an interrupting hand. "Again, these are corporate's marching orders, not mine. So take your complaints to them." He shooed her out of his office as a call came in. "I need to take this. Mic's Magic Show reported that they're missing their tiger. They told the cops that if anyone spots the big cat, don't harm him because they need him to perform in tonight's shows." He lifted his phone but placed his hand over the receiver as he continued in a softer voice. "If there really is a tiger on the loose, I'll need you to do a cut-in so we can notify the public. Put Tegan on it."

"I've got Tegan on the tank story."

"Then pull Patty off whatever she's working on and get her over to the neighborhood around the Luxor. The police seem to be focusing on that area."

Payson nodded as she shuffled out the door. The possibility of a tiger roaming a Las Vegas neighborhood wasn't holding her attention near as much as the news of a temp. She wasn't in the mood to spend the next several days with some lacky from corporate. She slumped in her chair, tossed the notebook on her desk, and stared at a fresh stack of papers that had appeared in her absence. She fanned her fingers through printouts of the day's national stories about death and destruction. *Why can't everyone just get along? For one freaking day?* Couldn't humanity just play nice so she could take a break from reporting the dark side and write about the nice things happening in the world? She stared again at the brochure of the tropical retreat and sighed.

The police scanner perked up, and she cocked an ear to the chatter. She caught enough of the exchange between officers to understand that a tourist had apparently decided to go for a swim in the Bellagio's lagoon. Police were being dispatched to the scene, and she knew a crowd would soon gather to witness the spectacle. If she could spare a photog, she'd send one over to grab a few interviews and hopefully get one or two good sound bites. If not, there would be plenty of video from tourists that she could obtain to fill a thirty-second spot in the A-block.

She grabbed another muffin, pulled off the top, and woke her computer. To those visiting the city and tuning into the local news, the stories would probably seem totally bizarre. To Payson, it was just another day in a town that seemed to attract the weird, wacky, and wild. "Viva Las Vegas, baby," she muttered under her breath. "Viva Las Vegas."

CHAPTER THREE

I'm going to be a temp? At a news station? I don't even know what that is." Hannah sulked as she slouched on the couch in Oriana's cottage. Most of the residents on the island chose to live in apartment-style dwellings close to town. A few, like Oriana and Hannah, enjoyed the solitude of being on the outskirts and closer to the woods, and their homes were only a five-minute ride apart.

"I consulted with a trusted friend who is well-versed in this culture, and she informed me that the fastest way to place you with your mark—and with the least number of questions—is to have you become a temporary employee. She has already called the television station and informed them that you will be assisting your mark in her business. You need to correct your mistake." Oriana paced around the room, her irritability obvious. "You, of all my students. Your mark was easy, a clear shot in a parking lot. A parking lot!"

"I got…" Hannah hung her head in both shame and embarrassment as she mumbled. "Distracted." How could she possibly tell Oriana the real reason? That a woman with eyes the color of Nikita's ring pierced her heart with one glance?

"*Distracted*?" Oriana overemphasized the word. "The island's best archer six years running doesn't get distracted. Have you learned nothing from me?"

Hannah kept her head down as she searched for the right words to convey her sorrow. But no such words presented themselves, so she silently listened as Oriana ranted. She had never seen her in such an agitated state, and it bothered her to think she was the cause of so much disgruntlement. After a beat, Oriana stopped pacing and let out a long sigh as she stood in front of Hannah. "Since you successfully placed the first arrow in one mark, you must make sure that woman kisses her intended companion. The kiss will transfer enough of the binding spell to seal their destiny."

"Get them to kiss?" Hannah jerked her head up. "But the attraction will only be one way. Can't Piper recreate a matching arrow so I can go back and finish what I started?"

"The arrows must be crafted together because the magic that binds them only responds to the spell of its companion. Even if Piper fashioned another set, a double dose of magic delivered in the one mark would be too much for her to handle. No." Oriana began pacing again. "For now, the only way around this is for them to kiss. You must make sure this happens."

"Oriana, I can't—"

"You must," Oriana interrupted. "I have faith that you will bring them together. Call upon the guidance of the laws of attraction to help steer them toward each other. All they need to do is kiss, and the binding spell will take care of the rest."

Hannah nodded. The laws of attraction she knew well. It was the lure that had led her down the road to many a lustful night. But to call upon that same magic to guide others down that path was beyond her abilities.

"Meanwhile," Oriana said. "I have already arranged for Dafina to take your place while you're gone. She will be discreet, and no one will be the wiser."

"Dafina?" Hannah spit the name out as though it were laced with poison. "You can't be serious? Dafina's an understudy."

Oriana gave her a knowing nod. "Well, for the next..." She waved her hand. "However long, she'll be a cupid." Oriana placed her hands on Hannah's shoulders. "The sooner you fix this, the sooner you'll be home. Worst-case, you fail to bring the two together, and the binding spell dissipates. If love is meant to be between them, their names will reemerge in the night sky, and another set of arrows will be crafted for them at a later date, when all traces of the original magic have worn off in the first mark." Oriana gently patted Hannah's shoulder, even though the twitch in her face gave away the anger still brewing within her. "I have faith in you because I have learned that when you put your mind to something, you are unstoppable."

Hannah nodded. She was grateful that Oriana was keeping this a secret from her fellow archers and that she was being given the time to discreetly fix her mistake. But an understudy performing her duties? She swallowed the acidic burn of bile bubbling up her throat. She was Hannah, best archer the island has ever seen, and now someone who couldn't even make the cupid cut was taking her place. "When, uh..." She trailed off as her mind raced with this new reality. She knew she'd be the laughingstock among her peers if ever this news made its way to the island's grapevine of gossip. "When do I leave?" she said in a faraway voice as she grappled with disbelief.

"Immediately. I've entrusted Piper to pick out appropriate attire for you to wear while you're amongst the mortals. She's waiting for you at your house."

"I see," Hannah choked out. Of course Oriana would need to tell Piper, who would now have to turn her arrows over to Dafina. A twinge of jealousy emerged as she thought about Piper sculpting arrows for anyone but her because they were not only best friends, they were an inseparable team.

"Now," Oriana said. "You must be off. I expect you to be successful in your mission and be back shortly. And Hannah, be careful while you are there, for mortals can be very unpredictable. Sometimes, they're not what they seem."

A chill shivered up Hannah's spine from the ominous warning, and Oriana's impactful lessons from her childhood emerged from the back corners of her mind:

"Mortals," Oriana said as she stood over Hannah and a seated group of a dozen young archers. "If your calling is that of a cupid, you will not only aid their love, you will be witness to many fascinating aspects of their cultures. You may even be tempted to befriend one. But be warned, there is a reason for our one law that strictly forbids them from ever setting foot on this island and why we encourage those islanders who encounter them to never linger in their company. Although we share many things with our fellow mortals, there are many more that separate us."

Oriana locked eyes with each student. "There was once a time when mortals lived amongst us and shared in the celebration of love, laughter, and craftsmanship we enjoy on this island. It was a harmonious relationship, and one that seemed to be beneficial to all…until the uprising, when many lives were lost, and betrayal lurked in the shadows."

Oriana's movements turned more dramatic as she reenacted the story. And although Hannah had heard her tell the tale many times, she was still glued to every word. The details changed a bit, but the premise was the same. A handful of island mortals decided to steal as much as they could of the gold that was mined for cupid's arrows. The nuggets netted them a sizable fortune. But instead of being content with what they stole, greed took hold, and they returned with a group of armed mercenaries in the hope of taking control of the island—and its abundant goldmine—away from Nikita.

A battle ensued, and many more mortals joined the rebels as they stormed the palace. There were deaths on both sides, including Nikita's childhood best friend, but in the end, the islanders managed to save their land. Nikita was so furious about the blood that had been shed and the life that was lost, she had all those who were not of island blood cast off the land, and the memories of this place wiped from their minds. She then instructed the spell makers to cover the island in a magical dome, making it invisible to the rest of the world.

"Mortals," Oriana said as she ended her story. "Put their love for greed over their love for this land and its people. They destroyed the balance and harmony. The island's land and all its inhabitants would have suffered in their hands if the uprising had been successful. Be careful around a mortal." Oriana pointed a finger at each of them. "For some bow to the good of self over the good of others."

"Then why do we give them the gift of love?" a fellow archer asked.

"Because it was the agreement Nikita made with the universe long before the uprising, and even though the mortals brought heartache and loss, the queen has never gone back on her word. And because of that, we will always honor our role and give the magic of love to anyone whose names light up the night sky."

And it was because of that story that Hannah had first viewed mortals with biased judgment. But as she and Piper became teenagers, curiosity had gotten the better of them, and they'd both wanted to experience what life was like outside the island. Piper had just begun learning her teleporting spell, so they'd thought, why not practice on themselves? And unbeknownst to their teachers, they had sneaked away to random places in the world, if only for a moment, to witness all the fascination and diversity life had to offer. And that meant mingling with the mortals.

And although they'd witnessed the results of devastating wars and horrible suffering, they'd also seen great acts of kindness and compassion. Not all mortals were as Oriana had portrayed them to be. Most seemed just as mesmerized by the wonders of life as she and Piper were, and it made them question if the law to forever ban them from the island was fair.

"I promise to be careful, and I will do as you wish," she said as she rose, clasped bracers with Oriana, said her good-byes, and began to walk back to her cottage. She could have whistled for Bella or teleported; after all, the clock was ticking down on the binding spell, but she was in no hurry to begin her quest. What had started out as a triumphant day was ending in epic failure.

How could this have happened? She replayed the moment she released the arrow and came back to the same frozen frame. Those eyes. They were magical and must have cast a spell of their own on her. She'd seen green eyes before, so why were these eyes any different? There was something about those eyes that "saw" her, as though there was a connection. But how was that even possible?

And not only that, but something else was gnawing at her. She was confident that even though she'd hesitated in releasing the arrow, her aim shouldn't have been *that* much off its mark. If not for that sudden gust of wind, she was convinced her arrow would have made contact with its target. Was the wind—her friend since she was a child—mocking her in some way because she hadn't listened when it whispered? Hannah shook off the thought. Impossible. The wind would never betray her like that. She always took time out of every day to honor their bond. She respected her place among all of the elements, and always tried to walk through her life without inflicting harm. No, she dismissed the previous thought, the wind would not forsake her. But even so, the thought of that sudden wind surge nagged at her.

As soon as she arrived at her cottage, she saw Piper's Palomino grazing in the field off to the side. She released a long sigh as she pushed through her front door. Piper was sitting on the couch, feet on the coffee table Hannah had carved from a fallen tree, drinking a mug of beer. A second mug sat untouched. "Thought you might need a drink." Piper slid her legs off the table and pushed the mug toward Hannah.

Hannah shrugged the quiver off her back and gently placed it and her bow on a shelf in the corner of the room. She let her fingers linger over both and remembered the day Oriana had taken her to see the island's master bowyer. He'd welcomed her into his shop and had enthusiastically introduced her to several of his already finished bows. He'd told her to try them out while he'd observed her stance and the way she'd gripped and balanced each one. She remembered his quick inhale when she'd transferred the bow with ease back and forth to each hand, firing off arrow after arrow. And he'd listened when she'd sadly turned to him after he'd asked what she'd thought and told him that none of his bows "spoke" to her.

"The balance is off when I shift from hand to hand."

"Ah." he had said with glee in his eyes. "That's because your bow has yet to be made. Give me a week, my child, and you will be united with the bow that will more than speak to you, it will sing in your hands." When she'd returned to his shop a week later, he'd looked up from his counter, smiled, and told her to give him a moment. When he'd returned from the back room, he was holding the most beautiful bow Hannah had ever laid eyes on. The combination of the dark wood that mixed with streaks of lighter, bleached grain caught her eye. The moment he'd handed it to her, a tingle had shot through her.

"Go on," he had said with a tilt of his head. "Take it out back and try it out." But Hannah had already known that this bow would be with her for as long as she could shoot an arrow. And true to his prediction, he'd crafted her a bow that sang in her hands and had never once failed her.

She gave the bow a loving pat as she turned, rounded the coffee table, and sank onto the couch next to Piper. She threw her head back against the cushion and let out a long breath. "What a disaster." Since becoming a cupid, she had never known the lonely feeling of failure until that moment.

"Care to share?" Piper raised her brow.

Hannah folded forward and scrubbed her fingers through her hair in frustration. "I don't know. It was weird. Right before I released your arrow, the mark, she, um, she glanced up and looked at me. It was as though we connected in a way I have never experienced before."

"Mortals can't see you while you're performing your duties," Piper said matter-of-factly.

"I know, that's what makes this whole thing so odd. But I'm telling you, she saw me. She stared right at me, and I could tell by the look in her eyes, she knew I was there."

Piper took a moment as she cocked her head in what Hannah interpreted as disbelief. Hannah couldn't blame her. If she had not witnessed it herself, she would never have believed her own story. But it happened. It was real. And Piper could believe her or not.

A blink later, Piper smiled in a dismissive way and slapped her on the back. "Well, if what you say is true, then whaddaya know? A woman finally caught the heart of the great cupid Hannah. You must tell me more about this mystical mortal."

Hannah shrugged out of what she felt was a condescending hand on her shoulder as she grabbed the mug of beer. She took a moment to take a sip before answering. "I know none of this makes any sense, but I'm telling you, she has eyes the color of Nikita's ring, and when she looked at me, I felt a wave of peacefulness surround my heart. I have never felt such a beautiful sensation." Hannah turned. "She saw me, Piper."

Piper searched her eyes as though they were wandering down many different roads, as if looking for a sign that Hannah might be messing with her.

Hannah held her gaze. "I'm telling you, she *saw* me. We stared at each other, and it was beautiful."

After a long moment, Piper nodded. "Well, if I wasn't so certain, I'd say you've been pierced with one of my arrows."

Hannah let out an uncomfortable chuckle. "What are you suggesting?"

"That you, my friend, are in love."

Hannah threw her head back in laughter. "I am not in love. Lust, perhaps, but she's a mortal, and I don't even know her. I was momentarily distracted, that's all." Piper's suggestion was both comical and unnerving. Hannah had plenty of women on the island to satisfy all her needs, and love was never part of that equation. Not to mention the sheer improbability of actually falling in love with someone without the use of a cupid's arrows. Love at first sight was the stuff of fairy tales, those stories and legends that were always spoken with whimsical tones and theatrical gestures. None of it was rooted in reality, at least not her reality.

"Well, whatever it was, I have faith you will be able to fix it."

Hannah frowned. That was exactly what Oriana had said to her, and unfortunately, she did not share the same faith in herself. "Have you ever heard any whispers of any other time this has happened to a cupid? And if so, how'd they fix it?"

Piper lifted her head as if in thought. "Nope. I think you're the first."

"Great." Hannah snorted as she bowed her head in shame. Cupids were never supposed to miss. That was why the annual competition singled out the exceptional archers from the rest. To claim cupid status meant there was an expectation that love's arrow would always hit its mark. "I'm afraid Oriana has sent me on an impossible quest, one I'm sure I'll fail at." First the failure of a runaway arrow, and now the inherent failure of an impossible task. Hannah wasn't sure what force shifted in the universe that day or what planet went into retrograde, but she sure wished that whatever it was, would shift back.

"If Oriana sent you, she has faith in you."

Hannah snorted. "Or she's trying to teach me a lesson."

"Well, I guess we'll never know her true intentions." Piper stood and helped Hannah off the couch. "But remember this, whatever is meant to be will be."

"And if I fail at bringing these two together in love?"

"Then the night sky will realign and send their names to Danika once again, and I will craft another set of arrows. So don't worry, one way or another, they will come together in true love. Meanwhile," Piper said as she led Hannah into the bedroom, "your new outfit awaits you. It's just like what they wear at the place you're going, so you'll fit right in."

"I seriously doubt that." Hannah sat on her bed and examined a pair of black jeans and a white button-down shirt.

Black boots sat on the floor by the foot of the bed. She stared at the outfit, and her shoulders sank. The costume looked stiff and restrictive. She glanced at Piper and tried to plead with her eyes. Did she really have to wear such clothing?

Piper gave her a knowing nod of encouragement and through a defeated sigh, Hannah began to slowly remove her clothes; modesty between islanders was never an issue. The naked body in all its forms was revered and admired, never shamed or criticized.

With shaky hands, Hannah picked up the pants and slid her legs into them. The fabric stretched around her muscular thighs as it encased her legs and seemed unbreathable and itchy, and she did several knee bends to test its flexibility. She grunted her disproval. Next, she began to shrug into the cotton shirt.

"Wait." Piper held out a lacey bra. "I think this goes on first."

Hannah took the bra through pinched fingers and kept it arms-length as though it was a rotting carcass. "What's this for?"

"You wrap it around your breasts."

"Why?"

"I'm not quite sure, but it's a clothing custom for women."

Hannah glanced at her chest. Her breasts were small and unassuming. Why in the world would she have to bind them? She crunched her nose as she brought the bra toward her for closer inspection. "I don't want to wear this."

"You won't have it on for long. I expect to see you back here very soon."

"I still don't want to wear this."

Piper took the bra and guided the straps up Hannah's arms, the cups around her breasts and hooked the back. "Well, like it or not, it's what they wear."

"It's itchy," Hannah said as she wiggled her upper body and scratched at her breasts.

"Well, hopefully you'll get used to it. Now then…" She handed Hannah the shirt. "Try this on over it."

"Fine." She huffed as she shrugged into the long-sleeve shirt. Her shoulders drooped under its imaginary heavy weight, and her hands were cold and clammy as she buttoned it up. The fit was a bit snug, but it accentuated her body beautifully. "It doesn't fit well," she said as she turned to Piper.

"That's because you buttoned it wrong." Piper approached, unbuttoned the shirt, then started from the bottom and worked her way up. "There," she said as she reached over and cuffed each sleeve. "Now then." She glanced at Hannah as she gently unclasped one of her two arm guards. "You will have to leave these here."

"No…please," Hannah pleaded as she placed a hand over Piper's. "I'll be lost without them. Look." She unrolled the sleeve. "I can hide them."

"Sweetie." Piper gazed at her with sympathetic eyes. "Oriana gave me strict orders that your bracers must be removed. You need to blend in, Hannah. With solid gold cuffs on your forearms, you'll attract the wrong kind of attention."

"But without them, how am I going to get around? I'll be grounded." All cupids had the same teleporting spell that Piper had learned woven into the silver inlay on their bracers. All Hannah had to do to activate the charm was place her first two fingers on each stripe, and the freedom to come and go off the island was hers.

"I'll get you there and back, no worries."

They stood for a moment, eyes locked in a standoff, until finally, Hannah lowered her head and nodded her defeat. She shed tears as Piper gently removed the guards from her forearms and tossed them onto the bed. Hannah rubbed the exposed skin that made her feel self-conscious of her body for the first time.

Hannah hugged herself as she slumped on her mattress. "How is it that I can split a pea in half over a hundred yards out, and I missed a person standing still in a parking lot?" And again, she felt the sting of betrayal from the wind. None of this was making any sense. The logic in her world was unraveling faster than she could adjust, and the pit in her stomach was rapidly becoming an endless well.

Piper sat next to her. "I don't know, but I wouldn't let it haunt you. Just keep your mind on what you need to do, and don't get distracted."

Hannah snorted. When she was a child, she would try Oriana's patience because according to her teacher, she lacked focus. "You are too easily distracted, Hannah." Oriana would tell her. "If you are ever going to be a cupid, you must learn to master your focus." But repeating the daily drills and disciplines that Oriana put them through was boring:

It was the same routine every morning. After a hearty breakfast with her fellow students and a morning of vigorous calisthenics, Oriana called them into the arena and had them practice their archery skills over and over. "Again," Oriana would bark after they shot the cluster of arrows in their quiver. "Again," she would repeat as she walked behind them, correcting inaccurate forms and sloppy postures. She would preach about focus and talk about being one with the bow. But by the time lunch came, Hannah became fidgety and more times than not, forwent a meal and used that time to run through the forest, swim in the lake, or dance with the butterflies in open fields. On a few occasions, she let her distractions get the better of her as time evaded her. Upon her return to the academy, she would try to sneak in unnoticed, which was virtually impossible to do under Oriana's uncanny, hawk-like vision.

One particular afternoon, she'd fallen asleep watching the clouds entertain her with their artistic impression of animal formations. "Shit," she'd murmured as she sprinted back to the academy and peered through an opening in the side arena door. When she saw Oriana turn her back, she hustled to her spot in line and quickly shrugged on her quiver.

"Hannah," Oriana called in front of everyone. "I will not have any student of mine make such a mockery of the ancient rules of discipline. I have had enough of your truancy. It is time you left this academy." The words stung as they slapped Hannah across the face. She had never meant to make a mockery of the ancient art of discipline. She was just someone who easily got bored and distracted by the many wonders of the island.

"Master Teacher Oriana, I beg of you. It won't happen again. I just fell asleep in the field."

"There's always an excuse." Oriana approached her and squared off. "Fell asleep, lost track of time, couldn't find my way out of the forest. It's always something, isn't it, Hannah? Well, let me make life easier for you. You are now free to run in the fields all day long or spend as much time as your heart desires in the forest because as of right now, you are no longer a student at this academy." She leaned in. "Go…now!"

Hannah's body swayed from the punch inflicted by those words, and she had to take a step back to maintain her balance. Disbelief swirled in her head as the room blurred, and her senses became hyper focused on Oriana's unflinching stern expression. A queasiness churned in her stomach, and the bitter taste of bile coated her mouth as she stood waiting for a sign from her master teacher that signaled she was teasing. Surely, she must be joking, right?

"You, uh…" Her voice cracked and caught in her throat. "You don't really mean that, do you?"

Oriana's brow arched as she stared her down. "Don't I?" she said as she crossed her arms.

Hannah nervously exhaled as she gazed again at Oriana, waiting for the usual, don't do that again, speech, followed by the tilt of her head that signaled Hannah should take her place in line next to her fellow students. But when none came and she realized that this time, her master teacher had meant every word, her knees began to buckle.

"I…" She trailed off as her mind went blank, and words jammed in her throat. "I…" she repeated as tears flowed down her cheeks. The academy was her home. Leaving it would be walking away from all she had ever known. And without Oriana's teaching, how would she ever make cupid? "I'm… sorry." She choked, and her throat constricted as she tried to say the words. "Please, Master Teacher…please. I won't—"

"I said, go." Oriana's expression was unwavering.

Hannah took a moment to gather her thoughts and her bow and began to shuffle away from the arena, her fellow archers, and a skill that felt more natural to her than walking. But before she left, she wanted to have the last word. And because the lump was still stuck in her throat, she decided to speak in a language Oriana could understand.

Hannah spun and fired off three arrows before most people could blink. Each one struck the dead center of the target, the subsequent arrows splitting the one before it. She switched hands and fired off several more, then sprinted toward a pole, jumped off it, and catapulted into the air. Before her feet settled back on the ground, she had fired the remaining arrows in her quiver. She stood defiantly as she gave Oriana one last look. She didn't bother to glance at the target like everyone else;

she could tell by their expressions what she already knew. She tried hard to keep her head held high as she nodded a painful good-bye to Oriana.

As she turned and walked away, Oriana called, "And where do you think you're going, young lady?" Hannah smiled as she stopped but refused to turn around. "Get back in line and give me twenty pushups, then a dozen quivers worth of shooting." Oriana clapped her hands. "Everyone, you heard me, or do I need to repeat myself?"

Hannah scurried back to her designated spot, hit the ground, and began crunching out her pushups. Halfway through her set, Oriana approached, lowered herself to a knee, and bent over. "See, when you put your mind to it, you have exceptional focus. Better than my most advanced archers. *But be careful, my child, for one of these days, your distractions really will get the better of you.*"

Hannah sighed as Oriana's words echoed in her head. She leaned forward and placed her head in her hands. She grunted in frustration as she scrubbed her fingers through her hair. "What happened to me?"

"Nothing happened to you. You were distracted. Something you have been your whole life. Only this time, it was a woman instead of nature that caught your attention."

Hannah scoffed and again thought about the wind. Something was tickling the back of her mind. Again, she replayed the release of the arrow. Yes, she had been distracted and yes, she'd released it in haste, but again, her aim was there, she was sure of it. How could the arrow miss so completely? "The wind," she whispered to herself. That odd gust that had blown through the moment her fingers had released the string. It was as though she were a child again, and the wind was trying to get her attention. And like before, she had no clue what it was trying to tell her.

"Well, fear not, you will be back before you know it." Piper scooped up both bracers and placed them on Hannah's dresser. "They will be here waiting for you when you return."

"Promise me, Piper. Promise me you'll take care of Bella for me while I'm gone." Hannah pleaded as she looked up.

Piper smiled as she approached. She stood over her and cupped a hand under her chin. "Bella will be fine, and so will you. You're not going into battle. You are going to unite love. You're a cupid, my friend, the island's best, and for the next day or so, you'll be doing what you were born to do. Just without your bow or arrows."

"Then this is ridiculous."

"No, it's not. You will figure out a way to get them together, and you'll return triumphant, and we'll celebrate over at Brea's. Now, come on, Oriana has instructed me to make sure I get you there on time. They're expecting you."

Hannah stood, scratched again at the bra, then held her arms out. "Well, do I look like a temp?"

"I'm not totally sure what all temps look like, but I can assure you that you look incredibly sexy," Piper said as she took a step back. "Now." She reached in the leather pouch slung on her shoulder. "This should be enough of their local money to get by while you're there." She handed a wad of American currency over to Hannah, who promptly shoved it in her front pocket. "Also, in case you have not succeeded by the end of tonight, you have reservations at a place called Gimbauld's Hotel and Casino. Here's their information. It's walking distance to where you'll be temping, so no need to worry about how to get there." Piper handed her a piece of paper. "Okay, I think that covers it. Are you ready?"

Ready? No, she wasn't even close to being ready. Ever since she was five and held that bow in her hands for the first time, her life had taken a predictable path. It had followed a series of well-laid-out steps that had led her to where she was today. But this—whatever this was—was never a part of that plan. How could she possibly be victorious if she was stripped of the tools and means that she had always relied on to succeed in her mission? No, this truly was an exercise in failure, and as she glanced at Piper, her confidence faltered. Shooting an arrow in someone from a distance was one thing, being up close, stripped of magic, and trying to manipulate love between two souls was something completely unnerving. "Piper…I…"

"You've got this, you'll be fine. We've been around mortals enough to know that they're nothing like Oriana portrays."

"I know, it's not that, it's more that I feel unprepared. Like I absolutely have no clue what I'm doing."

"Yeah, well, I feel that way with half the spells I create. Trust me, you'll figure it out as it goes. Now come on, the sooner I get you there, the sooner you can come home."

"Okay…" Hannah took a deep breath. "I guess I'm as ready as I'll ever be." She extended her hand, knowing that in order for Piper to teleport them to the location, she had to have physical contact when the spell kicked in.

Piper shook her head. "I can't escort you on this one. I need to send you there by yourself. I have a ton of stuff I still need to get done before tonight." Piper untied the small leather pouch hanging from her waist and poured white, chalklike dust into her hand. "Remember, once the two women kiss and the binding spell is complete, I'll come get you. But if by the end of the third day, they haven't kissed, then the binding spell will dissipate, and I'll pick you up at sunrise. But I have faith that I will see you soon." She blew the powder on Hannah. "Oh, and let me know how the teleport goes. This is actually a new spell I'm trying out."

"Wait. What! Piper, reverse the—" Hannah stopped midsentence when she noticed her hands turning transparent. Her heartrate jumped, and fear gripped her for a moment as she sensed a slight tingle of discomfort.

"Don't worry, you'll be fine." Piper's hollow voice sounded like she was at the bottom of a well. "I'm pretty sure I mixed everything right."

Hannah glanced down and focused on the few remaining visible particles of her body as the air was pushed out of her lungs. She tried to take a breath, but her chest constricted, and a suffocating feeling kicked in. A scream came from within but never made it to her lips as she glanced one last time at Piper before the darkness took hold.

CHAPTER FOUR

A jolt to her legs caused Hannah to stumble forward and crash into a wall. She groaned in pain and slowly regained her balance. As she rubbed the soreness from her shoulder, she made a mental note to tell Piper her spell definitely needed tweaking.

"Oh, good heavens." An older woman from behind a corner desk gasped. "You startled me. I didn't hear you come in."

Hannah jumped and spun in a circle as she blinked in a small room with red fabric chairs scattered around. Framed posters displaying several smiling people positioned in the same pose covered an entire wall. Opposite that was an oversize wooden desk where the woman now staring at her sat.

"You, um…you can see me? All of me?" Hannah glanced down as she ran her hands over her body.

The woman chuckled. "Of course, I can. Now, then, how can I help you?"

"Am I in…um, is this Las Vegas?"

"Last time I checked it was. Welcome to Ten on your side, Vegas's number one local news station."

"Huh." Hannah let out a breath. "It worked," she muttered as she checked her body once more to make sure she was intact. "I'm Hannah, and I'm the new temp for…" She paused as she searched her mind for a name she did not recall ever being given. "For, um…" She felt like saying she was here for the woman with the most enchanting eyes she had ever seen. The one who could make her heart flutter every time she closed her eyes and conjured up the image of the moment when she'd felt they connected.

"Payson," the woman filled in. "Yes, she notified me that you'd be arriving. She's expecting you. Please take a seat while I let her know you're here."

Hannah nodded. "Thank you." As she headed for a chair, she glanced at the poster-size photographs that graced the wall as though they were gods and goddesses to be worshiped. And there, in the middle of the group, displaying her pearly whites in an over-exaggerated smile was a face Hannah recognized as the woman from the red Mercedes. "Madison Morrison, evening anchor," she mumbled as she read the plaque under the photo while scratching at her bra. "Okay, Madison Morrison, time to get you and Payson together so I can go home, get out of these clothes, and get on with my life."

"Hannah?" a soft voice called.

Hannah turned and stared into the beautiful eyes that had caused this mess, and just as before, she felt warm calmness wash over her as she caught her breath and stood frozen. It was one thing to look into those eyes from a distance. Up close, where Hannah could see the way the slight variations in hues sparkled and blended together, was like looking at a hypnotist's pocket watch.

"It's you." Payson gasped. "Did you…were you on the roof across the…" She pointed to a spot somewhere behind her as her words trailed off. "I don't suppose you own a bow and arrow?"

Payson confirmed what Hannah already knew. She *had* seen her on the roof. In all the years she'd been performing her duties, not once had any mortal been able to see her. Visibility only came at her discretion. So how could this woman have looked through the dimensions and veils of magic and singled her out when she herself had not wished to be seen?

"A...um..." Hannah trailed off as she stood transfixed, feeling no need to break the trance between them. Payson was gorgeous, and as long as she could remember, when she came upon something that mesmerized her, she studied every inch so she could burn the image forever in her mind. "A bow and arrow?" She tilted her head as she brushed the question off as absurd.

Payson shook her head as she waved in front of her. "Never mind." She extended her arm. "I'm Payson. Nice to meet you."

The moment Hannah curled her fingers around Payson's hand, a shiver shot up her spine. She gently squeezed Payson's hand as she continued to hold the attention of those piercing eyes that had landed her in this predicament. "Very nice to meet you too."

"Well, um..." Payson slowly slid her hand out from Hannah's, tucked a loose strand of brunette hair behind her ear, and averted her eyes. "Please, follow me, and I'll show you to your cubicle." She stepped aside and held the door.

"Thank you." The subtle scent of lavender mixed with rose hovered in the air as Hannah stepped around Payson and into the building. She thought about rainy days on her island, when the flowers released their fragrant smells, and she smiled.

On their short journey through the hall, Hannah met several coworkers. All of whom seemed courteous and polite, and none of whom she committed to memory. Why should she? Her interaction with these people would be short-lived. A moment in time where their paths crossed and nothing more. As they rounded the corner and entered the newsroom, Hannah recoiled. It was a large open space with dozens of low-walled cubicles pushed together. If she squinted hard enough, she could barely make out the almost colorless gray paint on the walls. Fluorescent lights hummed overhead and overpowered the little amount of natural light trying to seep in from a few small windows. And as they walked past the assignment desk, a loud screech blared, causing her to place her hands over her ears.

"Sorry about that," Payson said. "I keep telling them to turn the police scanner down, but Jason insists it stays turned up so he can hear it. He's our news director." She motioned with a nod to the corner office. "So he kinda rules the roost when it comes to stuff like that."

"I see." Hannah shuddered as a slight headache began knocking at her skull.

"And here we are. This is my desk, and I thought it'd be best if you take the one right behind me. I grabbed a few things out of the supply room, but let me know if you need anything beyond the standard stuff." Payson extended her arm as she guided Hannah into the cubicle behind hers.

Hannah stood with slumped shoulders as she looked at the small, perfectly square space. An assortment of office items graced the desk, and she couldn't help but sigh over how pathetic the tiny area looked. She let out a breath and took another glance around the room as she tried to soothe the feeling of despair filling her stomach. The environment was sterile, dreary, and lacked anything that would feed her soul. The air was recycled, no natural light touched and nourished her skin, and there wasn't any nature to interact with. Not even the tiniest plant graced a single desk.

She felt claustrophobic. And even though she knew she was free to walk out at any time, she still felt caged. How did people exist in an environment like this, she wondered as she approached a chair that looked like it had seen better days? The chair rocked back as she sat, and she reached for the desk to prevent her from flipping backward. Payson grabbed her hand, setting off the same warmth and calmness as before. A one-time feeling of such intimacy, Hannah could reason away as an anomaly. But twice was something that definitely caught her attention.

"Sorry about that. I thought they fixed this chair. Hold on." In one quick motion, Payson helped Hannah up and swapped the chair out for another. "Here, let's try this one." She patted the mesh fabric as though testing it for firmness.

Hannah cautiously sat, leaned back, then nodded her approval.

"Payson," a raspy voice called out. "Payson!"

Payson rolled her eyes. "Yeah, yeah, I'm coming." She turned back to Hannah. "Jason's bark is worse than his bite, but trust me, he can still be a real pain in the ass," she said as she gestured to Hannah's cubicle. "Make yourself comfortable for a few minutes, I'll be right back."

Hannah nodded as Payson grabbed a notepad, shuffled into the corner office, and shut the glass door behind her. Jason's arms moved in an animated manner as Payson sat and began scribbling in her notepad. The dynamic between them was obvious from the moment he'd called Payson's name, and it rubbed Hannah the wrong way. She curbed an unexpected protective urge to storm into his office and get up in his face about his rudeness. But she reminded herself that the customs here were unfamiliar, and maybe his was a tolerated behavior. And besides, Payson was not hers to defend.

"Stay on task," she whispered to herself as she let the uneasy feeling of being an outsider settle in. "I shouldn't even be here," she mumbled through a frustrated breath as she scratched her back against the chair to alleviate the annoying itch from the bra. She rested her head on the back of her chair, used the balls of her feet to spin in a circle, and distracted herself by staring at a variety of water stains on the ceiling panels. By her third rotation, she was bored and fed up with the bra. She unclasped the hooks, reached up her shirt and ripped the fabric from her body. She let out a sigh of relief as she deposited it in a desk drawer. She didn't care if it was their custom to bind the breasts, the fabric was uncomfortable, and she couldn't concentrate with it on.

From the corner of her eye, she caught the young man at the assignment desk staring at her, mouth agape and phone frozen halfway to his ear. She nodded in his direction and was entertained as he tripped over himself and tried to reengage in his task at hand. "Men." She chuckled as her eyes traveled from him to Payson's cubicle. She scanned the equally confined space until she settled on a picture of an island waterfall. She sighed and wished she was home, where she felt at ease, surrounded by people she related to and in a place that made sense to her. Hopefully by the end of the night, she would be back, and she could put this embarrassing mess behind her.

She glanced toward the corner office. Payson had stopped writing and was robotically nodding as she sat in her chair. She really is extraordinarily beautiful, Hannah thought as Payson turned toward her and tucked a strand of hair behind her ear as she smiled. Hannah smiled back, then closed her eyes and let out a breath. She was enchanted by Payson; that was undeniable. Had Payson been an islander, she would have acted on her emotions. But the combination of Payson being mortal and already spoken for conflicted with her desires. Payson was forbidden fruit. Her destiny was with Madison, not Hannah. Sadly, the only role Hannah would ever have in her life was that of a matchmaker. Nothing more.

"Stick to the plan," she groaned to herself. "Stick to the plan."

"Well, that was less than entertaining," Payson said as she returned, tossed the notepad on her desk, ran a hand through her hair, and sighed.

"Is there anything I can do?" Hannah asked with concern as she noticed the new stress lines that creased her face.

Payson shook her head. "Nope…it's just another day in paradise," she said with bite. "Anyway. I need to get ready to—"

"Okay, I'm off to the…well, hello there," a woman said as she approached Payson's cubicle.

"Hannah, this is Tegan, our best reporter and the only person in this place who keeps me sane," Payson said.

"Yep, that's me, reporter extraordinaire and keeper of sanity. Also known as her best friend," Tegan extended her hand. "And you're here because…"

"I'm Payson's temp." Hannah smiled even though the words tasted bitter on her lips. If Oriana wished to teach her humility with this quest, then she was succeeding. She had been stripped of everything she identified with, and now she was even stripped of her title.

Tegan turned to Payson. "The grouch got you a temp?"

"Are you kidding? It would never dawn on him to perform an act of kindness. Hannah came from corporate. Some experimental project they're trying out. She's just here for a few days."

"Only a few days? Well, that's disappointing, but…we'll have to make the best of those days, won't we?" Tegan winked.

Hannah averted her eyes as she felt warmth flush her face. Tegan was cute and seemed confident, characteristics she found not only attractive but were usually a recipe for an evening of lovemaking. But in this particular case, the emotion that warmed her face was not laced with lust but more of unexpected bashfulness. An overtly flirtatious gesture in front of someone Hannah was attracted to made her a bit uncomfortable.

Payson cleared her throat. "You came by to tell me something?"

"Um…oh yeah." Tegan released Hannah's hand. "The tank story is legit. The cops escorted it off the strip, and it's now sitting in some neighborhood just north of the Strat. The scene is still unfolding, so I'll head over, grab a few interviews, and send you some B-roll and a couple sound bites for a tease."

"Actually, send me a twenty second look-live, and I'll need it by five thirty. Since I'm going to do a cut-in with Patty on the tiger from Mic's Magic that got loose, I'd rather fill your promo slot with the same feel."

"You're kidding." Tegan snorted. "A tiger got out? How'd that happen?"

"Don't know, we're still tracking the story."

"I have an ex who works for that show. I'll reach out and see if she can give us some behind-the-scenes info," Tegan said as she retrieved her cell phone and started texting. "I'll let you know if she has anything to share."

"Thanks, Tegan. Now go be the amazing reporter that you are."

"Yeah, totally amazing, that's me. Guess that's why I get paid the big bucks," Tegan said sarcastically. "Anyway, off I go. It was very nice meeting you, Hannah. I hope to see you later for drinks." She waved as she headed out the door.

"Drinks?" Hannah raised a brow.

"We go out for drinks after the newscast to decompress. Trust me, you'll understand why after we're done with the show."

"Do all of you go?"

Payson shook her head. "Me, Tegan, a couple of the guys from master control and engineering…oh, and Madison, one of our evening anchors, joins us from time to time. It's only for about an hour, but some stay longer and gamble."

Hannah knew firsthand how the effects of alcohol aided in decision-making when lust was in the air. If both Payson and Madison were drinking tonight, Hannah would be home before sunrise, she was sure of it. "Well, then, I can't say no to that."

"Great. Now, I need to start building the rundown for the newscast, so I guess you can just shadow me and let me know if you have any questions."

"Sounds good."

The rest of the afternoon, Hannah sat under the flicker of fluorescent lights, hunched over a desk, staring at a computer screen, and listening to the constant screech of the police scanner in the background. What made her a bit nauseous and overpowered her senses didn't seem to bother Payson in the least. In fact, she seemed to thrive on the environment. She juggled phone calls, answered endless questions from coworkers, screened video feeds from sister stations and national outlets, and wrote story after story on her computer. The pace was frantic, but Hannah had to admit, she was impressed at how Payson could juggle multiple tasks at once while keeping calm and never showing a single sign of aggression.

And just when Hannah was about to suggest they take a break to go outside and enjoy the fresh air or sit and relax while listening to the serenade of the birds, the back door opened, and the hairs on the back of her neck stood up. The air in the room shifted, and she was keenly aware that everyone got a little quieter. No, not quieter, more like on edge as Madison Morrison sauntered into the room clutching a Styrofoam take-out container.

Oriana had taught Hannah from a young age to pay close attention to any shift in energy. "Your surroundings will tell you when something's off. When that happens, you must listen." Oriana had told her. "Assess the situation quickly and never for a single moment doubt your senses, no matter what your eyes tell you, for looks can be deceiving. Something that can be beautiful and alluring can still bite, sting, or have hidden thorns."

Oriana's words echoed in Hannah's head as she gazed at Madison and winced. Her heels clicked loudly on the tile as if commanding attention, and her hips swayed as they fought for movement in the restrictive skirt that was tightly wrapped around her thighs. Her face was smooth but painted with more makeup than Hannah thought tasteful, and as she walked to her cubicle, she scanned the room without moving her head the slightest inch, something Hannah had seen predators do before they pounced on their prey. The woman was pinging all of Hannah's *danger* senses, and she knew that Madison Morrison was someone who could not only bite and sting but could do it with a smile.

CHAPTER FIVE

Hannah sensed Payson become a little bit fidgety when Madison strolled over. She couldn't tell if the shift in body language was a result of a shy attraction or intimidation.

"Payson," Madison said without looking up from her phone. "Do you have the information on the rancher in Phoenix that I'm supposed to interview for the…" Madison trailed off as she glanced up, cocked her head, and stared at Payson.

Hannah lowered her head, but from the corner of her eyes, she continued watching Piper's binding spell settle in. And although the magical attraction was one way, Hannah sensed from Madison's behavior that it would be enough to at least generate the desire for a kiss if not more.

"His name's Karl Johnson," Payson said as she handed Madison a folder. "All the information on his ostrich ranch is in here." She tapped the binder. "I'm giving you a minute and a half for the interview, and I'm throwing it at the top of the B-block. But heads-up, there may be a last-minute shift to one of the stories in the A-block. We have a tiger missing from Mic's Magic Show, so depending on how that plays out, I may have to shuffle a few of the stories around, but I'll let you know."

"Uh-huh, yeah, no worries. Thanks." Madison took the folder as she maintained eye contact. "Did you, um…did you do something different with your hair?"

Payson patted her head as though checking for any runaway strands. "No, why?"

"Huh. There's something definitely different about you today."

"No, just the same little ol' me." Payson fidgeted, then glanced toward Hannah. "Oh, hey, this is Hannah, my temp assistant. Hannah, Madison…Madison, meet Hannah."

"Wait, what?" Madison snapped as if blinking herself out of the trance. "You got an assistant?"

"Well, it's only for a few days, but yeah, Hannah has been assigned to help me. Corporate's trying out some new program with rotating temps that—"

"Jason!" Madison cut Payson off as she stomped toward the corner office. "I want an assistant too. How come Payson gets…" were the last words that lingered in the newsroom before the glass door slammed shut.

"She seems intense," Hannah said as she continued to stare at the spectacle unfolding in the office. So much for her hope that Madison would be a perfect match for Payson. What did the universe see in the pairing of these two women?

"Yep, that's Madison," Payson replied as she stretched in her chair. "Hey, you hungry?"

Hannah's stomach had been growling for hours. "Yes."

"Did you bring anything for dinner?"

"No, I didn't know I had to."

Payson glanced at the digital clock by the assignment desk. "There isn't enough time to run out and get anything. Come on." She shuffled out of her cubicle. "I always have an extra stash of veggie and bean burritos in the freezer. When it's this close to the show, I really need to be at my desk."

Hannah nodded as she followed Payson into another square room that was a smaller version of the one they'd just came from. Instead of cubicles, it housed a set of two round tables and chairs, a refrigerator, microwave, and coffeepot. The blue tinge of the fluorescent lights created the same sterile look, and Hannah wondered if every room in the entire station lacked color, character, and charm. She let out a breath as she walked over to the coffee pot, grabbed it, and sniffed the liquid.

"I wouldn't recommend drinking that sludge. I'm sure it's been sitting out for hours. If you want a cup, I'll make a fresh pot."

"No, that's okay." Hannah recoiled as she looked at the dark-colored liquid that had an oil slick floating on the top and placed it back in its holder.

Payson grabbed two small packages, ripped them open, and threw them in the microwave. She pressed a few well-worn buttons, turned, and leaned against the counter. "Tell me a little about yourself."

A knot grew in Hannah's stomach. Although she and Piper had enjoyed being amongst mortals while eating, drinking, and celebrating in a variety of settings, she had no interest in having a personal conversation with one. She only engaged with them from an observer's viewpoint, a stranger who was just along for the ride and had no intent on sharing even the simplest of intimacies. "What um…" She tried to clear the nervousness from her throat. "What would you like to know?"

"What do you do when you're not temping? Where're you from? Do you have any pets? You know, the usual interrogation stuff."

"Well, um, let's see. When I'm not temping, I work for a matchmaking service that's—"

"Wait. Hold up. You work for an online dating site?"

Hannah chuckled. "Well…kinda." She had pierced the hearts of many who'd participated in those sites. Unfortunately, many more of those hearts remained untouched by her arrows, their profiles unseen by the night sky. "But we tend to provide a one-on-one service, and we guarantee the match will end in love. Unfortunately, we can't guarantee how long that love will last."

"Wow, that's a pretty bold company statement. You'll have to let me know who you work for because I've been toying with the idea of trying one of those sites. But I just can't seem to—" The ding from the microwave interrupted her. "And that's dinner." She grabbed a couple paper plates and transferred a burrito to each. She handed one to Hannah. "Careful, it's hot."

Hannah stared at the pathetic looking blob of folded dough and wondered what the hell Payson expected her to do with it. She sniffed, then poked at the tortilla. "What is this?" She held the plate out to Payson.

"A burrito. Don't you like them?"

"Normally, I do, but this odd-looking thing is not like any burrito I've ever seen."

Payson nodded. "Yeah, I guess it is rather pitiful," she said as she cocked her head and motioned for them to leave. "But they're not half-bad."

Hannah followed Payson out of the breakroom, down the hall, and back to the newsroom. The entire time, she kept her eyes on the unmoving blob that rested on her sagging paper plate. When they returned to their cubicles, Payson took a big bite. "You really don't have to eat it if you don't want to," she mumbled as she chewed.

"We're eating here? At our desks? Wouldn't you rather go outside and enjoy the fresh air?"

"Are you kidding me? We don't have time for that. I always have a working dinner."

"Oh, I see." Hannah sank into her chair, tossed the paper plate on her desk, and glanced toward the back door. She rubbed the clamminess off her palms and onto her jeans. The suffocating feeling from being inside a building for so long was beginning to feel a bit unnerving. Never in her entire life had she been so absent from nature. She let out a shaky breath as she glanced again at the burrito. Maybe her anxiety had more to do with lack of food then lack of the outdoors. She pulled the plate over for closer observation and unwrapped the tortilla. A smashed dollop of some unrecognizable filling sat on top a spoonful of white rice. She bent and cautiously touched her tongue to the filling and recoiled. "It, uh," she said as she sat back. "It seems that I'm not quite as hungry as I thought."

"That's okay. I'm sorry I don't have time to get us something more substantial. But you can go out and get something for yourself, if you want."

As enticing as that thought was, Hannah knew that the moment she walked out of the building, she would never want to step back inside. "No, that's okay. I'll be fine." She stretched her neck to relieve some of the tension. Hopefully, Payson and Madison would kiss tonight, and she would be nestled in her front porch hammock before sunrise.

"Okay. Well, um, why don't you roll your chair into my cubicle so you can look over my shoulder while I finalize tonight's rundown."

Hannah did as she was told. "Is that you?" She pointed to one of three items tacked to the prefabricated wall as she settled her chair behind Payson. It was a photo of a smiling young girl standing between two adults.

"Yes, I was ten. Those were my parents. They both passed away when I was in college. A wrong-way driver hit them head-on late one night when they were on the freeway. I'm an only child, so in a split second in time, I lost my entire family." Payson gazed at Hannah. "Sorry, didn't mean to get heavy." She waved her hand and averted her eyes. "But I, um…I don't know. I just feel comfortable talking to you, hope that's okay?"

Hannah felt unnerved and excited that Payson seemed to trust sharing such personal information with her. "Yeah, it's totally okay. I'm just sorry for your loss," she said as she thought about her parents. Both were alive and still thriving. She saw them frequently, but truthfully, she felt closer to Oriana then either her mom or dad. And although she too was an only child, her fellow archers took on the roles of brothers and sisters. She felt fortunate that on Archer Island, the definition of family reached well beyond the biological.

Payson nodded. "Thanks. It's been many years, but there isn't a day that goes by when I don't think about them."

Hannah let a respectful moment pass before she asked, "And who's that little one?" She nodded toward a picture of a small dark brown terrier mix.

"That was Kona. I lost her last year. She was almost eighteen." Payson touched her finger to the print and outlined the top of Kona's head as though she was in a far-off memory. "Do you have pets?" she asked in a soft voice as she grabbed her burrito and took another bite.

"I have a horse. A Friesian. Her name's Bella," Hannah answered with pride.

"I've always wanted a horse," Payson mumbled.

"Then why don't you have one?"

"Because I can't afford one but mostly…work."

Hannah nodded. Of the three things Payson had chosen to tack on her little cubicle wall, two were of loss. "And that." Hannah pointed to the pamphlet.

Payson untacked the brochure, opened it, and handed it to her. "Ten days on a tropical island with nothing but women." She tapped a picture of a small group dressed in bikinis, laughing around a pool with colorful drinks in hand. "I was supposed to be there this Monday morning. I had money down and everything. But I guess it just wasn't meant to be."

Hannah glanced at pictures of a variety of women enjoying food, drinks, water, and land excursions in a setting that reminded her of her home. "Why aren't you going?"

"Because we're short-staffed right now, and Jason said he needs me here." Payson gestured at the newsroom. "Until we can hire another producer. With budget cuts, staffing keeps getting pushed aside as he spends the money on other things. So until then, I'm stuck."

Hannah's heart broke for her. Archer Island had a dozen cupids and a handful of understudies who were available at any given time. Hannah could take time off whenever she wanted, but she never did. She loved everything about being a cupid, and she'd never once wished to leave it all behind in exchange for a few days spent somewhere else. Archer Island nourished her soul, and her fellow islanders satisfied everything from friendships to sexual desires. She couldn't imagine living a life where she felt *stuck*.

"Anyway." Payson sighed. "One of these days, I hope to go. I could sure use some time in paradise."

"I hope so too," Hannah murmured as she glanced at Payson. She would love Archer Island, Hannah thought as she watched Payson stare at the brochure. Granted, it didn't have a group of women parading around in bikinis, huts that served tropical drinks, or a pool with a built-in waterfall and slide, but it had everything she thought Payson would love. If not for the law forbidding mortals on the island, and the fact that Payson was destined to be with Madison, Hannah would whisk her away and introduce her to what true paradise was really like.

How fun it would be to introduce her to Bella. Or to swim with her in the lake and then lie out on the bank under the warmth of the sun. Or to sit still in the forest long enough to let nature present itself. But to make that happen, she would have to go against the very reason she was here. No, she thought as she shook her head. Payson would never know the beauty of the island because her destiny was here with Madison. And it was up to Hannah to make sure *that* future was the one that happened.

"Huh." Hannah grunted as she was taken aback by her own thoughts. She had never once entertained the idea of bringing a mortal to the island. Why would she? She had never shared even the slightest meaningful conversation with one until now.

Payson gently tacked the brochure back on the cubicle wall as though the paper alone held a magical power that could teleport her to the place. And as she patted the photo of little Kona one last time, Hannah sensed not only a kindred spirit, but someone that she'd really like to get to know.

"Okay," Payson said as she shoved the last bite of burrito in her mouth and rubbed her fingers on a napkin. "Time to get back to work." She began explaining all the ins and outs of stacking a rundown for the newscast. She described how the sections were referred to as blocks, designated by commercial breaks. How the first few minutes of the broadcast were the most important because that was where the ratings played a role, and the higher the ratings, the higher the amount they could charge advertisers.

"That's why," Payson continued, "I'll always lead with the most eye-catching, sensational stories we have."

For the next hour, the frenzy of phone calls Payson juggled increased tenfold. She restructured and rewrote the rundown twice over, and the number of times she was called into Jason's office was more than Hannah could keep track of. By the time they entered the small dark room next to the studio that was filled with television monitors and switch boards, Hannah felt exhausted.

"Welcome to master control. This is where all the magic happens. From here, we can dictate everything that goes on air. Grab a headset. You can sit next to me and listen in." Payson pointed as she sat and began flipping switches on a control board. Hannah took the seat next to her, slipped on the headset, and listened as random voices notified Payson that they were in position.

"Okay. people," a male voice said. "We're live in a minute and thirty."

Payson wrapped her hand around the mic on her headset. "Get ready for the wonders of live TV," she whispered.

Hannah nodded as the wall of monitors came alive with an assortment of images and video, all waiting for their turn to be aired.

"And five, four, three, two…cue, Madison," the same male voice said as an explosion of frantic pacing unfolded. The tank was a stunt that an elderly eccentric millionaire had pulled to propose to his twenty-something girlfriend. He'd rented it from a Hollywood prop house, shipped it out, and hoped driving it down the strip would get her attention. The tiger that had escaped was eventually found lounging in someone's backyard, the tourist who'd decided to do laps in the lagoon did it on a dare from his bachelor buddies in town for a wedding, and on and on it went. The monitors switched back and forth between anchors, reporters, and videos at a dizzying pace. By the time Payson pitched to the national news package—riddled with killings, destruction, and overall unrest—she felt nauseated. What happened to all of the love she and her fellow archers had spent centuries delivering?

"Well," Payson said as the credits rolled, and she removed her headset. "What'd ya think?"

"I think…" Hannah trailed off, her mind numb from trying to digest the bombardment of rapid-fire information. "I think I'm glad I work in the business that I do instead of this one." Her days consisted of encouraging the expression of love between two souls and enjoying a way of life that was calm and peaceful. She had seen enough from her travels with Piper to understand that they lived in an isolated bubble that was void of such unrest. It wasn't in her face on a daily basis like it was for Payson, and she couldn't imagine what that must be like. "Doesn't any of this haunt you?"

"Yeah," Payson said in a nonchalant tone as she motioned for Hannah to follow her. "It can be a bit daunting."

Hannah fell in line as everyone shuffled out of the master control room and into the studio. "I would say, nice show, people, but yet again it wasn't clean…" Jason trailed off as he stood at the anchor desk and read from a piece of paper. He called out those who missed their cues, the graphics that had been misspelled, and how each of them needed to "up their game." He didn't offer praise or thanks, just criticisms and complaints.

Hannah found his mannerisms rough and his appreciation for what everyone did nonexistent. She quickly concluded that if ever his name appeared in the night sky, she would be tempted to break the companion arrow because pairing anyone up with him would weigh heavy on her conscience.

"So," Payson said as they returned to their cubicles. "You going to join us for drinks?"

"Of course."

"Great." Payson gathered her purse and led the way out to the parking lot. "We meet over at Gimbauld's, the casino just up the street." She pointed as she unlocked her car. "Meet us in the back lounge just past the keno room. You can't miss it."

Hannah nodded as she began walking out of the parking lot and up the road. The temperature was a little warm but pleasant. She took a moment to gaze at the stars, but unlike the sky that greeted her every night on the island, the stars here were hidden behind a layer of light pollution. How sad, she thought, to live a life without the brilliant display of the universe's art twinkling overhead. She thought about all the times she'd lain in the hammock on her front porch, swaying as she tried to read the night sky. She was not looking for the names of future lovers, like Danika was, but she sought the names of past ones. And wondered what their stories were and how each came together in love.

"What are you doing?" Payson's voice snapped her back to reality.

"Heading to the casino." She addressed Payson, who was leaning out of her open window. "Why, is something wrong?"

"Yes, you're walking. Something that isn't advisable around here at this hour. Where's your car?"

"I don't have a car," Hannah said nonchalantly. "Besides, it's a beautiful night, and it feels good to walk off all the sitting we did today." In fact, she had never sat so much in all her life, and her muscles ached from nonmovement.

"Didn't corporate provide you with a car?"

"No, I…uh, a friend made sure I got here."

"Ah…well, hop on in and ride over with me." Payson moved the papers and items off the front seat and tossed them in the back. "Sorry about the mess."

"No worries," Hannah said as she folded into the car seat.

"Okay, tell me the truth…what'd ya really think about the show?"

Hannah thought about her life. All she had to do was shoot an arrow into the heart of someone. She didn't set it up, make the arrows, or in any way coordinate the encounter. She just showed up and did her thing. Granted, she was the best when it came to archery, but it was only one task. She was awestruck by Payson's diverse talents. "I thought you were amazing. I don't know how you juggle it all without faltering."

"When I first started, there were four of us who divided the roles that now fall under my job description. Like everyone else at the station, I've learned to do more with less and figure it out as I go along. I'm not really sure how corporate expects us to wear so many hats and be good at them all. It's no wonder we make mistakes, and the burnout rate is so high."

Again, Hannah just nodded. What could she possibly contribute to this conversation? The burnout Payson alluded to was foreign to her. It was no wonder her arrows seemed to be less effective in binding some souls in long-lasting love if ancient spells had to compete with this type of modern stress.

"And now the question I've been dying to ask all day," Payson said, "is corporate's experimental program of rotating temps really just a ruse to spy on us?"

"I don't understand what you mean."

"We've all heard the rumors about corporate wanting to sell off the TV stations they acquired, so I just figured they're sending temps out to report back to them. You know, so they can justify getting rid of us. Not that that would be a bad thing. Corporate doesn't seem to know anything about managing news stations, but getting shuffled around to a different parent company usually never ends well."

"What's wrong with the company that owns—"

The tap of a car horn interrupted Hannah, and they both turned to the bright red Mercedes sports car sitting next to them. The passenger side, limo-tinted window powered down, and Madison leaned over. "Last one there buys the first pitcher." As soon as the light turned green, the Mercedes shot out of the intersection. It was a block down the street before Payson's car cleared the crosswalk.

Payson glanced at Hannah. "Guess I'm buying the first round."

"It appears so," she said as Madison's taillights faded into the darkness, and she wondered once again if there was a misread of the night sky. She had always considered herself somewhat intuitive—easily reading the flow of the air, movement of the seas, and whispers of the trees—but for the life of her, she couldn't understand why the universe had paired those two. Payson was beautiful, kind, and had a gentleness that…

"Oh my God, stop it," she quietly scolded herself. She needed to rein in her personal feelings and accept that there was a master plan in place that went beyond her understanding. Stick to the mission, she reminded herself as she turned to Payson. "Tell me what you think about Madison?"

"Not much to tell." Payson shrugged. "She was a morning reporter in Chicago with aspirations to be an anchor. So when Jason thought our one female evening anchor, who had been with the station for over thirteen years, was aging out, he replaced her with Madison. It's sexist because the male anchors in this business seem to have no problem growing old on air, but the women are time limited. But from a strictly ratings perspective, he was right. Our ratings have gone up since he hired her, so I guess there's that."

"What I meant was…are you attracted to her?"

"Wow, don't you think that question's a bit personal?"

"Sorry, I didn't mean to pry, but I'm pretty sure I felt something between you two today. I guess it's just the matchmaker in me noticing two people who would make a great couple." She felt like puking on her words, but this was no time for her honest opinion. She and Payson came from two different worlds, and right now, she really wanted to go home to hers.

"Well, it's funny you mentioned that. Because I, uh…" Payson blushed as she trailed off. "I kinda felt the same thing."

"See? I told you."

"Yeah, I mean, I really didn't think I was even on her radar. People like Madison could have anyone."

"Why do you say it like that? In such a dismissive way?" Hannah felt stunned. "I think you're a beautiful and kind person. Where I come from, you could have your pick of lovers."

Payson chuckled. "Wow, you're just right out there with your comments, aren't you?"

"I'm sorry. I didn't mean to sound so forward, but remember, I am in the business of—"

"Matchmaking. Yep, got it." She paused for a moment, then glanced over. "So, um…I wasn't totally crazy thinking there really was a certain vibe coming from Madison?"

"I think," she said through a forced smile, "there's something between you two that may be worth exploring."

"Oh, you do, do you?"

"Well, yeah, I mean, are you saying you're not into her?"

"Are you kidding me? She's gorgeous. Who wouldn't be attracted to her?"

Me, for one, Hannah thought. Madison did not possess any qualities she found endearing or remotely attractive. "That's not what I asked."

Payson remained silent as she pulled into Gimbauld's lot and parked.

"I'm just saying," Hannah continued as they crossed the parking lot and headed toward the entrance. "There's something between you two. I felt it." From the corner of her eye, she could tell Payson was turning the information over in her head.

"Well," Payson said as she opened the door for them. "I guess that's yet to be seen."

As soon as Hannah stepped into the casino, she cringed. The flashing lights, the dinging bells, and the lingering smell of stale cigarette smoke, might be stimulating to mortals, but it was completely overwhelming her senses.

"You okay?"

Hannah shook her head. "Why is everything so loud?" Granted, things could get a little rowdy at Brea's from time to time but nothing compared to the level of volume she was experiencing. It was as though the casino went to extremes to tune out the beautiful sound of silence.

"I really never noticed," Payson said in an over-amplified voice.

As they meandered through the casino, Hannah focused on the faces of the mortals. She could sense the desperation that lingered in the air and heard more of them whisper prayers to machines and tables than they probably did in any worship setting. As though the roll of the dice, turn of a card, or spin of a slot would somehow make all their troubles disappear.

"About time you showed up." Madison sat surrounded by a half dozen coworkers in a small semi-round booth. A three-piece band was performing a short distance away, and a server dressed in clothes more suitable for a beach headed to their table. Madison tapped the space next to her. "We've been waiting for our beer."

Payson smiled. "You going to hold me to that, huh?" she said as she slid next to her. Hannah flanked her other side.

Madison smirked. "Of course I am, you lost the challenge."

"The challenge was rigged."

"Never rigged, only slightly manipulated." Madison winked at Payson, who averted her eyes and blushed.

"What can I get you guys?" the server asked.

Payson spoke up. "We'll start with a pitcher of whatever you have on tap."

"You got it." The server smiled and left with their order.

"Sorry, I'm a little late." Tegan scurried up to the booth and slid in next to Hannah. "The pole attached to the satellite disc on the van got stuck and wouldn't collapse. Suffice it to say,

Jason's going to have a shit fit when he realizes what we had to do to get it down. Anyway, what'd I miss?"

"Nothing. We just got here," Payson reassured her.

"Oh, good." Tegan turned to Hannah. "So what'd you think of the show?"

"I thought your tank story was…entertaining."

Tegan lightheartedly laughed. "Yeah, and check this. What the viewers don't know is, when the cops told the guy to step out of the tank, the only thing he was wearing was a pair of tighty-whities, and a big ol' engagement ring was dangling from a safety pin attached smack dab in the middle of the underwear."

The table laughed.

Payson recoiled. "Ew, that's gross."

"I know, but apparently, his girlfriend liked it because she said yes. So there you go, a happy ending to another bizarre story."

The laughter morphed to *aww* as the server returned with their pitcher. "Give me a holler when you need more," she said as she turned and left.

Madison grabbed the pitcher and started pouring for everyone. When she handed a mug to Payson, her eyes lingered. "To our star producer and another successful newscast." Madison raised her glass in a toast, and the table followed suit.

Hannah took a swig and gagged. The beer tasted of sawdust and moldy corn, and she resisted the urge to spit. When she realized the only socially correct place to put the vile liquid was down her throat, she closed her eyes and painfully swallowed.

"Not a fan of beer?" Tegan asked.

"Not a fan of this beer, no." Hannah coughed.

"Yeah, it's not the best, but don't worry, the first mug you taste, the second you feel." Tegan nudged her in a lighthearted way.

Hannah had no intention of getting that far. She pushed the mug away, ran her sleeve across her lips, and silently cursed her situation. She was starving for food that stimulated her tastebuds and thirsty for a beverage worth swallowing. Between the shriveled-up burrito and the foul-tasting beer, she was unimpressed with the cuisine, or lack thereof, that this city had to offer. She rubbed her temples in an attempt to keep the low-grade headache that she had been nursing since her arrival at bay. She glanced at Payson and let out a defeated breath. As much as she thought her name should have been paired with Payson's in the night sky, Hannah was becoming cranky, frustrated, and just wanted to get the hell out of Las Vegas and back to where she belonged. She closed her eyes and silently conceded to the universe. She should have known not to second-guess destiny.

"She's single, you know," Tegan whispered.

"I'm sorry…what?" Hannah opened her eyes.

"Payson. I see the way you look at her."

"Oh." The feeling of exposure caused her to fidget. "Well, actually, I think she and Madison would make a better couple."

"Madison?" Tegan groaned. "Are you kidding me? That woman doesn't recognize anyone in her orbit unless they have something to offer her," she said in a low voice.

"Are you saying Payson can't offer her anything?"

"Nope." Tegan shook her head as she took another sip of beer. "At least not the kind of thing Madison is looking for."

"And what's that?"

"Anything that boosts her career and ego."

"What about love?"

Tegan choked on her drink. "That woman isn't capable of loving anyone but herself. Madison is as fake as they come, and if those two ever did get together, she would break Payson's heart."

Hannah's stomach bottomed out. Payson was a kindhearted soul and someone who she would take pride in being with. The thought of knowingly pushing her together with someone who would hurt her would haunt Hannah forever. Something about this whole thing just wasn't adding up. Hannah shook her head to clear the thoughts as she leaned forward in the booth, put her elbows on the table, and scrubbed her fingers through her hair. She needed to detach from the situation and from her own feelings. Madison couldn't be *that* bad, could she? And the universe couldn't be *that* far-off, could it?

"Move…move." Madison waved her hand as she shooed people out of the booth. "I need to use the restroom."

"Mind if I follow?" Hannah jumped at the opportunity to get a better read on Madison, which shocked her. She had never before given a mark a second thought, much less questioned the universe's pairing process. She had always assumed that by the time she received the arrows from Piper, all was as it should be.

"Come on, girl, follow me." Madison waved.

"So," Hannah said as she caught up to her. "Payson's really beautiful, huh?"

Madison raised a brow. "Um, yeah. And you're asking because?"

"Oh, I don't know. I just kinda thought—"

"Are you into her?"

"What? No, I was actually thinking about you. In fact, have you ever, you know…" Hannah shrugged. "Thought about asking her out on a date? Or even kissing her?" Okay, maybe that wasn't the smoothest way to help plant the seed or push the laws of attraction forward, but the clock was ticking down on the binding spell, and like it or not, she still had a duty to perform.

Madison's icy stare sent a chill through Hannah. "You know what, temp?" She stabbed a finger in Hannah's chest. "I think you need to mind your own business," she said as she pushed a stall door open, slamming it against the wall for added emphasis.

"Hannah. My name's Hannah. Not temp. And it was only an observation," she spat as she turned to walk out.

"Whatever," Madison mumbled.

Hannah heard the dismissive bite in Madison's voice and cursed herself for not paying more attention to Piper when she was practicing her magic. If ever there was a time she wished she could conjure a spell to blow up a toilet stall, this was it. What the hell did the universe see in this woman?

❖

An hour later, Payson yawned and announced, "I think that's it for me. Time to head home."

"You're leaving?" Hannah asked with disappointment. The past hour had been unexpectedly pleasant, and even though she was still leery of Madison, the rest of the group she found to be entertaining and nice. Surprisingly, she could easily see herself being friends with all of them.

"Well, yeah, it's been a long day. I'm beat." She gazed at Hannah. "You good, or do you need a ride somewhere?"

Hannah paused long enough to give her butterflies time to take a lap around her stomach, then settle. How was it that a single stare, the slightest touch of skin, or a smile could melt her so completely? "No need." She shook her head. "I'm staying here."

"You're staying here?"

"Yeah. Why, is this not a good place?"

"No, I mean, yes. It's fine. Definitely close to the station."

Hannah nodded. "Which is why they picked it."

Tegan wrapped Payson in a hug. "I'm going to enjoy another round with everyone, then play some cards. See you tomorrow?"

"Sounds good," Payson said as she broke the hug and stood. "I'll see you guys later." She waved as she began walking away. "Oh, and Hannah." She turned. "I'll see you at the station around one."

"Hold up, Payson. I'll walk you out." Madison scooted across the booth. "Move…move!" She snarled as she waved her hands. "See you later, losers." She chuckled as she stepped next to Payson, threw an arm around her shoulder, and escorted her out of the lounge.

"Bye," Hannah meekly whispered as she watched them disappear into the vastness of the casino. She lowered her head, and a sinking feeling washed over her. If she were in Madison's shoes right now, there would be no doubt this evening would end with a kiss and a hell of a lot more. The thought caused her heart rate to soar as the urge to sabotage her own mission bubbled to the surface. She blew out a long breath as she tried to calm herself. Let it go, Hannah, she told herself. Let *her* go.

"You okay? You seem a little agitated," Tegan said.

"I, um…" Hannah tried to clear the dryness from her throat as Oriana's words echoed in her head: "I'm counting on you to fix your mistake and come home." But was the mistake really on Hannah, or was the mistake on the universe? She felt her chest tighten and her stomach bottom out as she began to think the unthinkable.

"I gotta go." She scooted out of the booth. Something deep in her gut told her to stop the kiss and intervene in the universe's plan. "This is crazy," she whispered to herself as she paced in front of the booth while trying to reason with herself. On the one hand, she could be completely ostracized from the island if she interfered with their destiny, but on the other, she could be righting a wrong. "Shit," she whispered.

What was it about Payson that enchanted her so much that Payson's future wellbeing was of such concern to her? None of this was making any sense. In less than twenty-four hours, her world had been turned upside down, and a life that seemed as predictable as the daily rising of the sun was now in question. She didn't understand what was going on, but if the wind had taught her anything, it was that she needed to listen when something was trying to get her attention. And right now, it was her heart that was whispering in her ear. "I gotta go," she repeated as she habitually slapped her fingers on her wrist once, then twice, then glanced at her arms as the reality of not having her bracers to teleport sunk in.

"Um," Tegan said as she arched a brow. "You doing okay there, Hannah? Anything I can help with?"

"No, thanks," Hannah called over her shoulder as she hurried into the main floor of the casino. But anxiety gripped her as she tried to get her bearings. She had been so transfixed on Payson when she'd followed her in, she hadn't taken note of her surroundings. She spun in a circle as she scanned the sea of people and blinking lights. Where the hell was the exit? She weaved her way through the slots, past several tables, and ended up at a dead end in the sports bar. "Shit."

She spun again, but finding her direction without the aid of the stars or the sounds of nature to help her navigate was impossible. Everything about the casino seemed to be designed to keep someone in, not let them out, and she could sense the window of opportunity to stop the kiss was closing. In desperation, she grabbed a man's arm as he passed.

"Hey!" The man jerked back.

"The exit," she pleaded. "How do I get out of here?"

"I don't know." He took a step farther away from her. "Why don't you follow the signs?" he said as he pushed past her.

Signs…what signs? Hannah glanced around, then up. A placard with a list and several arrows, all pointing in different direction, hung above her head. She quickly scanned the sign until she saw the word she was looking for: parking. The arrow pointed to the right, so she sprinted in that direction until a beam of light, bleeding through a section of glass doors, guided her the final distance.

"Payson! Payson!" she called out as she ran through the sliding doors and down a row of cars. But it didn't take long to realize that something wasn't right. "No." She placed her hands on her head. "No," she repeated as she glanced around the parking garage. She let her arms drop to her sides as she hunched her shoulders and lowered her head. She was in the wrong place, and because of it, she was sure she had just missed another shot at sealing Payson's destiny.

Chapter Six

"Seriously? You self-parked?" Madison scoffed as she handed her ticket to a young man behind the valet kiosk. "Why in the world would you do that?"

Payson chuckled and thought about Hannah's reply when she happened upon her walking to the casino. "Because it's a beautiful night."

"What does that have to do with anything?" Madison snorted, then turned. "Yoo-hoo," she called. "Be extra careful when retrieving my car, it's a Mercedes." She returned her focus to Payson. "Why in the world would they have such young people parking such expensive cars? He barely looks old enough to drive. If there's a scratch or dent on my new baby, I'm suing."

"I wouldn't worry. I'm sure he's quite capable in his job."

"Easy for you to say, you drive a—"

Payson gave Madison a look that hopefully conveyed she would be skating on thin ice if she finished that sentence.

"I didn't mean anything. I'm just worried about my car and…" Madison waved a hand. "Never mind. Anyway, I actually got a little sidetracked from something I've been meaning to ask you."

"Oh?" Payson's voice raised an octave.

"What are you doing after the show tomorrow night?"

"Going home." Payson paused. "Why?" She smiled.

"Would you like to go to a late dinner? I'm pretty sure I can get reservations at Antoine Yves. They serve until midnight."

"Antoine Yves?" Payson let out a gasp. "I heard there's over a month waiting list to get into that place." When she'd first moved to Vegas, she'd aired a package Tegan produced on the multi-award-winning Michelin star chef whose culinary skills and unique menu were quickly becoming the talk of the town. It was not only *the* place to dine, but on any given night, there was sure to be at least one major celebrity sighting at the restaurant. If Madison was trying to make an impression, she was definitely succeeding.

"There isn't a waiting list for those who know Antoine." Madison winked. "So what'd ya say?"

A jolt of excitement pulsed through Payson. A dinner date with Madison Morrison at Antoine Yves? Of course, she was going to say… "Yes, oh my God, are you kidding? I'd love to."

"You're too cute." Madison chuckled, then paused as she tilted her head. "Then I guess it's a date," she said in a soft voice as she held Payson's gaze and slightly rocked forward.

"Yeah," Payson whispered back as she licked her lips. "I guess it's a—" The tap of a car horn caused her to jump.

"Your Mercedes, ma'am." The valet smirked as he held open the door.

Madison whipped her head around and glared at him. "Yes, I can see that," she said as she did a quick three-sixty around her car, overtly inspecting it. She nodded her approval, retrieved a dollar from her purse, and handed it to him.

Payson noticed a slight eye roll as he glanced at the bill before running back to the kiosk.

"Well, then," Madison called. "Guess I'll see you tomorrow."

"Yep, see you tomorrow." Payson waved as she watched Madison speed off and disappear into the neon glow of the night. "I have a date," she said as she stretched her arms and twirled. God, how long had it been since she'd had a romantic night out or even a good-night kiss? She couldn't remember. Oh, well, the math didn't matter; the answer her body gave was, *too long*. "I'm going on a date with Madison Morrison," she repeated with glee as she strolled to her car. The darling of the evening news had just asked her, a nobody, out for dinner at one of the most prestigious restaurants in town. Maybe, she thought as she glanced toward the sky, things are starting to look up.

As she drove away, her internal excitement remained, but the face in her mind soon morphed from Madison to Hannah. There was something about the new temp that intrigued her. She had a childlike innocence that was such a juxtaposition to the way she looked. Under that rock-hard body was someone who seemed soft and gentle. Someone who had set in motion both fantasies and butterflies. "Hmm," she mused to herself. She had known Hannah for less than twenty-four hours, yet the feeling of reuniting with a long-lost soul was definitely there.

She lowered her window and let the night air cool her thoughts. As the neon reflections of the town spilled over her windshield, her mind shifted to Vegas as Hannah's words from earlier echoed in her head. Why didn't she leave her job? Go somewhere where she had more time to enjoy life? Get another dog and take the vacations she so desperately needed? Maybe even move to a place where she could once again enjoy the four seasons. After seven years, sin city was no longer holding her attention. Lucky seven, she mused as she mindlessly drove over familiar streets. "Maybe it's time to cash out?" she muttered as she let her mind's autopilot not only drive her home but also steered her down the many roads of memories:

Payson was excited when she got the call that the Vegas station wanted to hire her. She had been the morning producer at a small southern Iowa station since she'd graduated from college. But it was a triple digit market, and in the game of broadcast news, the higher the number, the smaller and more dismissable the city. At market one hundred and thirteen, she was in broadcast Hicksville. Her life had become as stagnant as her job, and it was time to move on.

She gladly accepted the position, cashed in the small inheritance from her parents, and headed for the city of neon lights and new beginnings. But the town that had originally given her so much eventually took even more: her ex, Julie. They met while Payson worked on the station's annual fundraising drive for local school supplies. Every company donating five hundred dollars or more got a minute of free airtime to plug their business. On one particular fateful day, Payson was the one who escorted Julie back to the studio for her minute of fame as a representative for the construction company she worked for.

Two weeks later, they were an item, and three months after that, Julie moved in. The day Julie announced that she wanted to go back to school and finally get the master's degree she had put on hold, Payson was not only supportive, she offered to help out financially.

"I'd pay for it myself if I could," Julie told her on the heels of a sob story about how an ex had ruined her credit and had made it impossible for her to obtain a loan. Payson offered to cover the cost of her schooling by using her own credit cards. Julie swore through kisses that as soon as she graduated, she would become the breadwinner in the relationship, pay off Payson's cards, and take care of her.

But two years later, when Julie claimed that the university had made a calculation error in her credits and she needed

Payson to apply for an additional credit card to cover the cost of another semester, Payson's gut told her something was off. She asked Tegan to do a little digging into the situation and see if the university was bilking the students for additional tuition. But what Tegan uncovered was not fraud on the part of the university but a scam on Julie's part. Seemed she had never enrolled in classes at all, and the money that she had cashed out of the cards to cover her "tuition and school fees," was instead going toward a gambling addiction. The long hours Julie claimed to be putting in at the library were really hours at the tables.

When Payson confronted her, she denied it. But two days later, she came home to a house empty of Julie and her things. After all her years working in the news industry, writing story after story warning viewers about hacked accounts, scams, and email schemes, she herself had fallen victim to a con. For the next month, Tegan tried her best to track Julie down, but she had vanished off the radar.

"She ghosted out," Tegan told Payson. "She no longer exists in the data sources I have access to. At least not under that name."

Payson thanked Tegan for her efforts and told her to stop the search. She was exhausted from crying, hurt from the betrayal, and embarrassed every time she thought about it. Julie was gone, and she needed to close that chapter of her life and begin putting back together the shattered pieces of her heart.

And three years later, Payson had only just begun to make a dent in the debt. With her trust in relationships as bottomed out as her bank account, she'd poured what was left of her heart into the one love she had left: Kona. With her gone, Payson had lost the last bit of what seemed to matter the most in life: happiness.

She pulled into the garage of her modest-sized tract home. No soul was waiting for her to return, so the house greeted her with the quiet sound of loneliness. She threw her purse on the coffee table, made a cup of tea, and eased into a well-worn section of her couch. It was midnight, and she was feeling both wired and tired. She grabbed her remote and turned on the TV to overpower the silence. The distraction of voices at least gave her the false sense of not being totally alone. She flipped through the channels until she paused on a reality crime show. Her gaze eventually drifted to her end table and settled on the cluster of framed photos. She had once heard someone say that memories were the most dangerous form of heart disease, and as she focused on a picture of her mom and dad—smiling as though they hadn't a care in the world—she couldn't agree more. She kissed her fingers and tapped the frame of the souls she could never again hold in her arms, share her life's stories with, or tell over and over how much she loved them. A deep sadness took hold as her gaze drifted to a photo of Kona in her younger more vibrant years.

She tapped the top of her picture frame as well. "I miss you, girl," she said as she took another sip of tea and nestled deeper into the cushions. She should probably go to the shelter and adopt another dog. It would be good for her heart. But with the number of hours she was logging at the station, she didn't think that would be fair. Work was consuming her life, and for the foreseeable future, that meant not having a furry companion to come home to. Her primary relationship these days was with a job she was no longer in love with. She let out a breath, leaned her head back, and focused again on the screen as her eyes started to feel heavy. Date night on the couch with her TV was becoming the norm. It kept her company and was a good distraction from her life. A life that had become as empty as her heart.

Bored with what she was watching, she was about to flip the channel when a female cop appeared on screen, and Payson smiled. If not for the long black hair, the woman could be Hannah's twin. "Hannah," she said in a barely audible voice as a calmness settled in, and sleep began to take hold. Hannah was as easy on the eyes as she was to get to know. She exhaled a contented breath, and as she drifted asleep, she let the voices from the TV serenade her as her mind filled with images of Hannah.

CHAPTER SEVEN

Hannah sat slouched on a bench outside the south entrance parking lot, waiting for Piper. It had taken her five attempts to locate the correct parking area, and by that time, there was no sign of Payson. Now, all she could do was wait for the inevitable. Oriana and Piper would both be pleased to have her home, but as she shuffled her feet and became more fidgety, she knew that she would never be able to get the beautiful sparkling emerald eyes of Payson out of her mind.

She let out a frustrated breath. Damn the night sky and damn the universe for dangling the perfect woman in front of her while knowing she could never have her. No matter what her heart had whispered to her, she had to accept the fact that Payson's love might have truly been meant for another.

After an hour passed with no sign of Piper, then two, Hannah began to worry. Surely, Madison and Payson had kissed by now. How could they not? No, the delay must have been on Piper's end. Hannah knew how scattered she could be at times, so she waited…and waited. And when the same security guard drove his golfcart past a third time, asking her if he could assist her in any way, she decided it was time to head inside.

She reentered the casino and followed the now familiar signs to the front desk where she exchanged her name for a room key.

"Take the elevators around the corner. Your room's on the sixth floor, end of the hallway on your right," the clerk informed her with a smile.

"Thanks." Hannah nodded, rounded the corner, and as the doors to the elevator closed, she slumped as the weight of the day pressed on her. It was true that she missed the beauty of the island, the quiet of the night, the distant sound of the waterfall, and evening rides with Bella. But the heaviness that gripped her was more than that. She pondered it as the doors opened, and she meandered down the hallway. It unnerved her to know that there was a part of this place that she was going to miss. That through all of her grumbles and resistance about being here, there were actually moments where she felt like the city held a charm all its own.

She let out a sigh as she stood outside room 623. Who was she kidding? It wasn't this place that she was going to miss; it was Payson. She snorted at the irony of spending a day with the only woman who had ever truly caught her eye and then encouraging her to be with another. "You're such a wreck," she whispered to herself as she let her forehead fall against the door. As she was about to place the keycard in the slot, the door swung open, and Hannah lost her balance as she fell into Piper's arms.

"Piper." Hannah squeezed her tight as a lump rose in her throat, and a hollowness spread throughout her stomach. Piper's appearance was proof that the two would-be lovers had united, and Hannah's conviction that the stars were wrong was nothing more than her own fantasy getting the best of her. As she pulled out of the embrace, she did a double take as she glanced at Piper's outfit. "What are you wearing?"

"You like it?" Piper twirled in a pair of black leather biker boots as she displayed a yellow floral sundress that hung a little loose on her slim frame. "It's my mortal costume."

"I don't understand. Why would you wear a costume to come pick me up?"

"Pick you up? I can't pick you up yet. You know I'm under strict orders from Oriana not to bring you home until I get confirmation that the marks have kissed."

"But the marks left together hours ago. I've been waiting since then for you to bring me home."

"Really? The marks have been together for hours? Huh, that's interesting..." Piper trailed off as she grabbed the teardrop-shaped black obsidian stone necklace dangling halfway down her chest on a leather cord. "I placed a spell on my necklace so the stone would glow when their star lit." She gave the stone two taps and a shake. "Yep, still no glow, which kinda surprises me. There should have been enough of a spell on the one arrow for the attraction to have turned into action by now. Hmm." Piper shrugged and released her necklace. "Oh, well, there's probably a delay in the confirmation, it's happened before." She waved a hand. "Anyway, that's not why I'm here."

"Wait...back up. Are you saying they haven't kissed?" she said with hope.

Piper shook her head. "No, I'm saying their star hasn't been lit, *yet*. But give it a moment, the night's still young. It'll happen, I'm sure." Piper smiled. "Meanwhile, I figured that, while we wait for confirmation that their destiny is truly sealed, and before I take you home, we can do a little gambling. I've never been to this city that sins, and I want to see what it has to offer. I did some checking after I sent you here, and I understand they have some great card games, so I'm curious to see how challenging Vegas's mortal opponents can be."

Card games had been played on the island for hundreds of years, first introduced by the mortals and continued to be played by the islanders. Poker and twenty-one being the island's favorite. Both Hannah and Piper were skilled at the rules, and each considered themselves an excellent player. But of the two, Piper seemed to have an uncanny sense for the games. She could outplay almost anyone on the island, and Hannah wondered a time or two if the wind wasn't whispering its own lyrics in her ears.

"Do you still have enough currency?" Piper asked.

Hannah dug into her front pocket and displayed the wad Piper had given her as her mind raced with the latest news. Could there really be a delay in the star? Yes, of course there could. Piper was right, it has happened before. Madison was sure to have kissed Payson by now, and any other scenario just didn't make sense.

"Well, then, what are we waiting for? Let's go play." Piper smiled.

"I don't know, Piper, can't you just sneak me home, and we can wait for confirmation there?"

"Seriously? Wow, when did you turn so boring? Come on…" She hooked her arm around Hannah. "It'll be just like when we were younger and sneaking off to all the places around the world and hanging out with the mortals."

"I've hung out with them all day." Hannah groaned as Piper led her out of the room.

"Well, I haven't. Come on," she whined, "a few games. By then, the stone will surely be glowing, and I'll take you back."

"Oh, that reminds me. The spell you used to send me here needs tweaking. The landing was too hard, and it sent me into a wall." Hannah rubbed on her shoulder for emphasis.

"Really? Huh, I probably mixed in too much willow bark. Good to know."

As they stepped into the elevator, Hannah shoved her hands deep in her pockets, leaned back against the wall, and exhaled a long sigh. She gazed at Piper's necklace and willed it to glow because she knew each agonizing minute that ticked by while she waited for final confirmation of the inevitable was going to feel like slow torture.

"Oh, don't look so gloomy. The marks are probably getting it on right now. The star will light soon enough, and you'll be home, and back to your cupid duties by tomorrow morning. If you got them to leave together, then you did good, Hannah. You accomplished what you came here to do. Oriana will be proud," Piper said as she slapped her on the back.

Hannah forced a smile and nodded as Piper started filling her in on the latest island gossip. She wondered what Piper would think of her if she shared the news that she almost intervened with the universe's plan, and that she was convinced in her heart that she and Payson were the ones destined to be together. She glanced at her, then slightly shook her head. No, better to keep those feelings to herself. Piper wouldn't understand why she would want to deliberately sabotage the mission. To Piper, there would never be a question where her loyalty lay. And up until this afternoon, Hannah could have claimed the same.

As they walked out of the elevator, she focused again on the necklace as Piper continued jabbering on about Isabella wanting her to teach a class at the academy on arrow making. Hannah nodded and said all the appropriate things when prompted while never taking her eyes off the stone. Although it had yet to glow, she knew her time here with Payson was done, and that was a hard pill to swallow. Eventually, she hoped there would be another who made her body feel so alive, but for now, she knew it would take time to get the woman with the enchanted eyes out of her mind.

Their first stop was an unpopulated blackjack table. Hannah placed several bills on the velvet surface and was gifted with a tower of chips. She split the stack with Piper as a server approached. "Don't get the beer," Hannah warned.

Piper nodded. "Gin and tonic for me and..." She tilted her head toward Hannah.

"Actually, is there some place still open that serves food?"

"Honey," the server replied. "Everything's open. But if you want something fast, I suggest the café just past the craps tables. Order the truffle parmesan french fries, and you won't be sorry."

Hannah followed her line of sight and thanked her for the suggestion. "Here." She pushed her chips toward Piper. "I'm starving, so I'm going to grab something to eat. You going to be okay for a bit while I—"

"Hannah?"

A familiar voice caught her attention and she glanced around.

"I thought that was you," Tegan said as she approached. "Is everything okay? You seemed so upset when you left the bar."

"Yeah, no...I mean, yes, everything's okay. In fact, I was just about to..." Hannah trailed off. "Wait...you play cards, right?"

Tegan nodded. "I sure do."

"Then I'd like to introduce you to my best friend, Piper. Piper, this is Tegan. She works at the TV station I'm temping at."

"You're a card player, huh?" Piper asked as she motioned to the seat next to her.

"I am." Tegan sat and placed her drink on the table.

"Good, then let's get this game going." Piper smiled.

Hannah patted Piper's shoulder. "I'll see you in a bit, okay?"

Piper waved her hand. "Take as much time as you want. I'll be fine."

Hannah shuffled into the café and minutes later, slid into a small booth holding an extra-large plastic basket full of truffle parmesan french fries. She took a moment to glance around and was surprised by how many people were still out and about at the late hour. But in a place that displayed no windows or clocks, she could see how time played an elusive trick on the body.

She let out an exhausted breath as she focused on an elderly couple two booths over. The man was feeding soup to his wife and gently wiping her chin. That, Hannah thought to herself, is the face of love. She scolded herself for not knowing if she was the cupid who'd delivered their arrows many moons ago. She had never taken the time to commit the faces of her marks to memory, something she wanted to be conscious of doing from here on out.

Hannah remained mesmerized by the couple as she lifted a fry to her mouth. She bit off the tip, and her tastebuds came alive. "Oh my God," she whispered as she gazed at the shoestring food. The server was right; she wasn't disappointed. In fact, she was pleasantly pleased with the unique taste. What an interesting thing to do to a potato, she thought as she shoved handfuls into her mouth. It took her less than a minute to polish off the entire basket.

Her hunger satisfied, she leaned back in the booth and glanced once again at the elderly couple. That was what she wanted, a love that would beat the odds and last a lifetime. To wake up every morning and look into the eyes of her lover and know that their feelings would conquer anything life threw at them. That was what she had wanted with Payson.

As Hannah returned to the blackjack table with a new to-go container in hand, she zeroed in on Piper's dangling necklace. The stone was still black as coal, without the slightest hint of a glow, and she wondered what was taking the star so long to light. "Here, you must try this food. It's called a french fry," she said as she opened the Styrofoam container in front of Piper, who took a few and nodded her approval. "Tegan? Want some?" She motioned, but Tegan waved her off.

"These are delicious," Piper said as she reached for more.

"I talked to the cook at the café, and he told me how he made them. I'll share the recipe with Brea."

The clearing of the throat from the dealer brought the focus back to the table.

"Oh, sorry," Hannah mumbled. "Didn't mean to interrupt. I'll, uh…I'll be over there trying my hand at one of those machines."

Piper nodded, and Hannah approached the first video slot machine she encountered. She sat, placed the container of fries on the seat next to her, and took a moment to observe others playing the slots. After a few minutes, she convinced herself that it didn't seem too complicated, so she slid a bill in, pushed one of the many flashing buttons, and mindlessly watched cartoonish images spin in front of her as a disjointed jingle played from the machine. Seconds later, everything stopped, a multitude of lines appeared on the screen in endless configurations, and the flashing buttons prompted her to play again.

"That's it?" she disappointedly whispered. Unlike cards, there apparently was no skill required to the game beyond the basic coordination of pressing a button. Oh well. At least it would kill some time while she waited for Piper to finish playing. She leaned, head in hand, on the machine, yawned, and continued the repetitive motion. Red digital numbers went up and down with each push, and her eyes became heavier and heavier as she tried to focus on the spinning images.

"Hey, wake up," Piper said as she gently nudged her.

Hannah rubbed her eyes. "Is it time to go home?" she asked in a groggy voice.

Piper grabbed her necklace and dangled it in front of Hannah. "Still no glow, which is odd because by now, the star should have definitely been lit," she slurred and waved a hand. "But you know how stars can be. Sometimes they seem to have a mind of their own," she said as she stumbled a bit.

"Yeah." Hannah let out an annoyed sigh. Her body ached from falling asleep on the slot machine, and her heart ached from knowing Payson was probably in the arms of Madison. "Are you saying I'm still stuck here for a while longer?"

"Oriana gave me strict orders to—"

"Not bring me home until we have confirmation that the marks have kissed. Yeah, I know. Meanwhile, you're not going home either. You're too tipsy to navigate."

Piper waved a hand in front of her face. "I'm fine."

"No, you're not. Remember the last time we were traveling around the world and had a bit too much to drink in that one pub in Ireland?"

"That place had the best music." She smiled, then hiccupped.

"Yes, they did. But do you also remember that when it was time to go, you teleported us to three different locations around the world before you finally got us back home?"

"I did, didn't I?" Piper chuckled.

"Yes, you did." Hannah wrapped an arm around Piper as she led her toward the elevators. "That's why I think it's a good idea for us to go back up to the room and sleep for a few hours. You can sober up, and by then, we'll surely have confirmation from the stars."

"Yes, ma'am." Piper saluted, then handed Hannah a wad of cash.

"Holy shit. Piper, you did great."

"I'm going to keep some," she said as she slid several bills into one boot. "For when I come back. There're a few games here that I want to learn."

Hannah nodded as she wrapped an arm around Piper, walked her back to the room, undressed her, and gently placed her under the covers. She opened the curtains enough to make sure the sun woke them when it rose and stripped off her own clothes, glad to be free of the clingy, stiff material, and settled on her back next to Piper.

"I like it here," Piper said in a barely audible mumble.

"It has its moments, I'll give it that." Hannah clasped her hands behind her head and stared at the ceiling.

"Make sure…" she said through heavy breaths. "You wake me at dawn."

"I will," Hannah said as she heard Piper's breathing turn to a light snore. She closed her eyes and tried to settle her mind, but when thoughts of Payson and Madison together flashed in her head, a twinge of jealousy took hold.

She peeled the covers off, walked to the window and glanced out over the blinking neon lights. Somewhere out there in the vastness of the city, was Payson. She turned her gaze to the night sky and searched through the haze for a bright new shining star as she wondered if Payson and Madison really had kissed tonight.

She ran her fingers through her hair as she tried to calm her anxiety and hope. She had never in her life both wanted and feared the same outcome. If they hadn't kissed, she knew herself well enough to know she would probably try to intervene once again, and she also knew Oriana well enough to know what that meant for her cupid status. She sighed in frustration as she shook out a surge of adrenaline. She could probably lap this hotel five times over and not burn through it all. She twisted her upper body around and glanced again at Piper peacefully sleeping. Yeah, that was definitely not going to be her tonight.

❖

The sun shining in Hannah's face caused her to drape her arm over her eyes. She sleepily groaned as she rolled on her side. "Wait, what time is—" She sprang out of bed, rushed to the window, and peered through the opening in the drapes. From the position of the sun, she estimated that it was midmorning. "Shit." She hurried back to the bed and shook Piper. "Piper, wake up."

Piper waved her hand at Hannah. "Go away," she grumbled.

"Piper, it's midmorning."

Piper's eyes flew open, and she jumped out of bed. "What? Why didn't you wake me at sunrise?"

"I only just woke up myself," Hannah said as they danced around each other, grabbing clothes and getting dressed.

"Shit, Isabella's going to have my head if I'm late for this class."

"Did they kiss, Piper?" Hannah said as she shrugged on her clothes.

"What?"

"Your stone. I can't tell if it's glowing."

Piper paused, glanced at her stone, then stared at Hannah. "They didn't kiss."

Hannah's knees felt weak as her heart pounded with second-chance possibilities. "Are you sure?" she asked.

"Yes. The star would have definitely been lit by now. There's never been this much of a delay in confirmation. I'm so sorry, Hannah. Looks like you'll be here another day."

"Another day…" Hannah smiled as her stomach tightened with excitement.

"Wait a second, hold up. I know that look," Piper said as she sat on the bed zipping up her boots. "Please tell me you're not still intrigued by this mortal."

Hannah averted her eyes. "What? No, I, um…it's just that it'll be nice to see her again, that's all."

Piper approached Hannah and stared her down. "Don't even think about it. I'm serious, Hannah, don't go there."

"I'm not thinking about—"

"Yeah, you are. I've known you my entire life, and I can read you like a book. Your wheels are spinning, I can tell."

Hannah let out a sigh as she hunched her shoulders. "If you could feel what I feel when I'm around her. There's something between us, Piper. Something that whispers to me and says she's the one."

"What are you saying, the wind's now talking to you about your mark?"

"No, this is something that's coming from deep down in my gut."

Piper snorted in a dismissive way. "Look, I gotta go. But my advice to you, and I suggest you take it, is finish what you started and leave her be. You've already made one mistake by missing her with the arrow, don't make another. Especially one that you'll regret." Piper stood. "Listen to me. Hannah, don't do anything foolish and don't go chasing her." She snapped her fingers and disappeared.

"Yeah…sure." Hannah sighed. There was some truth in what Piper said, but damnit, it looked as if the universe was giving her a second chance with Payson. And because of that, today she would approach Payson and not hold her feelings back.

But as Piper's last words echoed in her head about not chasing her, she remembered a time when she was a child, running through the wildflowers in a field, when she'd seen a particularly beautiful butterfly. She'd chased it all day, wanting so badly to hold it in her hands and pet it, but the butterfly always flew away before she was able to capture it. When she'd told her mom about it over dinner, her mom had told her to stop chasing it. "If the butterfly wants to be friends with you, it'll come to you," her mom had said. "Sometimes, Hannah, chasing the things we so desperately want only scares them away. Next time, let the butterfly decide what it wants." And sure enough, the next day, when Hannah had sat calmy in that same field, the butterfly had eventually come to her.

And with a renewed sense of purpose, Hannah smiled. She'd give Payson her space, and let Payson determine what she wanted…and *who* she wanted. If Payson came to her, she'd have her answer.

CHAPTER EIGHT

Payson woke at dawn needing to pee, and by the time she returned to the couch, her mind had already done several laps around her day's to-do list. She rubbed the back of her neck and yawned. It was another reminder that she really needed to wean herself off the whole couch and TV crutch she'd developed in her latest bout of feeling lonely and sorry for herself. Add that to a job that was taking too much of a toll on her life and it was no wonder she had been feeling a bit melancholy lately. She lay there for a few more minutes, willing herself to go back to sleep, but her jumble of thoughts wouldn't release their grip.

"Fine." She huffed through a frustrated breath as she rolled off the couch. "I'll go for a run." She had been scolding herself for weeks for slacking off on exercising. Today would be as good a day as any to reset that routine.

The early morning air was already warm but thankfully, not yet blazing. And even though her body felt sluggish, thoughts about her dinner date with Madison sent a surge of well-needed energy through her. She settled into a comfortable pace and rhythm while her mind drifted once again from Madison to Hannah. There was something so enticingly alluring and organic about her, a definite connection that she'd felt from the first time she'd looked in her eyes and again every time they touched.

"Hannah." The name tasted sweet on her lips. "I don't know who you are or where you come from, but you're definitely the most interesting thing that has happened in my life for a long time."

Thirty minutes into her run, Tegan's name appeared on her watch. "Yeah?" she said through heavy breaths.

"You out running?"

"Yeah." Payson repeated as she rounded the neighborhood tree that signaled her halfway mark.

"Wanna get breakfast?" Tegan asked. "I can drive you back to your house afterward."

"Yes, I'm starving. Meet me at Bunches of Bagels in about twenty minutes. It'll take me that long to jog over there."

"See you then."

Her twenty-minute ETA took over thirty. She just couldn't shake the sluggish fatigue that had become her constant companion. As she opened the door to the bagel shop, she welcomed the smells of toasted bread and roasting coffee beans.

She ordered her usual, and five minutes later she settled into the chair next to Tegan, one hand wrapped around a cup of double-shot, almond milk cappuccino and the other gripping an egg and cheese bagel sandwich.

"How was your run?" Tegan asked.

"Horrible." She groaned. "My body just couldn't quite shift into gear."

"And that surprises you? After all the hours you've been working, it's kinda amazing you're still upright and functioning."

Payson took a sip of coffee. "I really need a new career." She exhaled and closed her eyes in a moment of Zen as she let the caffeine begin to work its magic.

"I heard Mandalay has an open marketing position," Tegan said.

Payson peeled an eye open as she tilted her head. “Oh, I don’t know. Part of me wants out of Vegas as much as I want out of news. But I’ll look into it though, thanks.” She grabbed her sandwich and took a bite. “Did you end up playing cards after I left?”

“Yep.” Tegan’s eyes lit up as she bent forward. “And guess who I ran into at the blackjack table late last night?”

“Who?”

“Hannah and her very delightful friend, Piper.”

A stab of jealousy and disappointment surprised Payson. As exhausted as she was last night, the thought of spending some leisurely one-on-one time with Hannah was appealing. “Delightful? Really? Do I detect a twinge of lust?” She raised a brow.

“More like a surge, but I wasn’t catching the same vibe from Piper. She seemed more interested in the cards.”

“Oh yeah? Is she as good as you?” Payson had been gambling with Tegan enough to know she could be a professional player if she wanted. She had never meet anyone who had such an intimate relationship with Lady Luck.

“Better. She cashed out at least triple what she originally had on the table.”

“Wow. Sounds like you’ve met your match. Did you guys exchange numbers?”

“No, but she did say she’d love to get together for a game of poker next time around. So there you go.” Tegan smiled.

Payson smiled, knowing that if Tegan and Piper did hook up, it would probably never last more than a few months, a year tops. It wasn’t that Tegan had a wandering eye; it was more that she had yet to find a girlfriend who shared in her love of gambling. Someone who understood the thrill of a card game and didn’t complain when she didn’t want to go home, sit in front of a TV, and do the homebody thing.

"Maybe." Tegan shrugged as she took another sip. "How about you? What'd you do after you left? I noticed Madison walked you out last night. What was that all about?"

"Well, guess who asked me out on a dinner date tonight?" Payson smiled.

Tegan froze. "Please tell me it's not Madison."

"Gee, don't act so happy for me. And, yes, Madison asked me out. She's taking me to Antoine Yves."

"Wow, that's um…Madison, huh?"

"Okay, first of all, you're a reporter who can pull words out of her ass at will, and that's all you've got?"

Tegan settled back and took a moment to finish the last of her coffee. "Look, sweetie, I know you've been kinda crushing on her a bit from time to time ever since she first came to the station, and it's not that I don't know what you see in that woman, but I really don't know what you see in that woman. I mean, don't get me wrong, she's gorgeous and all but seriously disturbed deep down."

Payson chuckled. "She's not *that* bad."

"I think the word bad is one of those relative words," Tegan said. "Look, I just want what's best for you, and I don't want to see you get hurt again."

"Well, Madison is no Julie, that's for sure."

"No, but she's also not good enough for you. Please don't fill your relationship void right now with another mistake."

"Ouch, that was a bit harsh, don't you think?"

Tegan placed a loving hand on her shoulder and squeezed. "I just want what's best for you."

Payson snorted at the catchphrase. She had been in survivor mode for so many years, she had no clue what "best for her" was anymore. She thought the tropical vacation she had booked was going to be a good start at finding that, but when it didn't pan out, the desperate feeling of her life falling apart once again took hold. But maybe it was for the best. How could she possibly think about her own self-interest when she had a massive credit card debt to pay off? She should just hunker down and not worry about herself until she fixed those loose ends. And even though she had contemplated bankruptcy many times to finally be rid of the bind Julie had put her in, she was too embarrassed and prideful to follow through with the paperwork. No…she'd gotten herself into this mess because she'd trusted someone. She could damn well get herself out of it.

Just keep your head down, do your job, and bit by bit crawl out of the rubble, she reminded herself. And maybe that wasn't what was *best* for her, but for now, it was the hand she'd been dealt.

She picked at her sandwich as she thought about Madison. If they did get together, would it *really* be such a bad thing? Madison's salary was probably two to three times what she was making. How refreshing it would be to be with someone she didn't have to support. Plus, she was beautiful and had a witty side. But on the flip side, she could also be cold and abrasive around the edges. Payson chuckled to herself. She was already making a pro and con list. As though tonight's date was really going to lead to anything substantial.

"You must be really enjoying that sandwich because you got pretty quiet all of a sudden."

"Sorry," Payson said as she refocused. "I was just thinking about the aftermath of Julie and promising myself to never get in a situation like that again."

"You won't because I won't let you. How much more do you have to pay off?"

"I have three more payments on the one card and more than I want to count on the other two."

"Well, as soon as I win the lottery, I'll pay off your cards, and we can run away to Mexico and live on the beach for cheap. We'll be the two mysterious lesbians everyone whispers about."

"Sounds intriguing."

"It does, doesn't it? And to think, the only thing standing in the way of our dream is six lucky numbers."

"And that, my friend, is why we'll be working stiffs for the rest of our lives."

"Hmm." Tegan reached over, grabbed Payson's sandwich, and took a bite. "Such a tragic thought," she mumbled as she chewed.

Payson smiled as she lifted her cup. "Well, at least we'll be in it together."

❖

An hour later, Payson was distracting herself with the long overdue task of cleaning her house. If her date with Madison went well, would the night end in her bedroom? She let out an uneasy breath as she stripped the sheets, replacing them with clean ones. Why was she so nervous about tonight? She had worked with Madison for almost six months now, so it wasn't like she was a stranger or anything. But still, spending time with her as a colleague and spending time with her on a date were two totally separate things. Or were her nerves about something else entirely? In the past twenty-four hours, she had experienced such a weird mix of feelings for both Hannah and Madison, she couldn't quite get a handle on it. Was she doing the right thing going on a date with Madison tonight when her mind kept drifting to Hannah? Her body at times said yes, yet her gut was screaming a totally different answer.

By noon, she was showered, shaved, made-up, and zipped into her best black dress. She checked herself multiple times, changed the color of her lipstick twice and her choice of shoes three times. Finally calling it good enough, she grabbed her purse and drove to the station.

As she walked into the building, she noticed Hannah sitting in her cubicle, head leaned back in her chair as she shot rubber bands at a stain on the ceiling that resembled a bullseye. Her sleeves were rolled up, and Payson could see the muscles in her arms flex with each movement. The butterflies took a few laps around her stomach as a vision of what those arms would feel like wrapped around her body emerged. As did her nipples, which were rock-hard and standing at attention. Payson glanced at her chest and rolled her eyes. Of all times to wear a sheer bra instead of one whose padding could hide her sexual arousal. "Great," she whispered as she shook her head and tossed her purse on her desk.

"I'd challenge you to a shooting contest, but we'd have to do it while Jason wasn't looking," she said to Hannah. "And I see you brought your dinner today." She pointed to two large Styrofoam containers sitting on Hannah's desk.

"I brought us both some french fries for…" Hannah trailed off as her gaze rolled over Payson. "You look absolutely stunning."

Payson felt the heat flush across her face as she tucked a strand of hair behind her ear. Granted, she was feeling sexy at the moment—and she was glad Hannah thought so—but that feeling was more a reflection of the dress and makeup and less of a reflection of her true self-image. "Thank you. I, um, I have a date with Madison tonight, and since she picked an upscale restaurant on the strip, I thought I better dress a little more appropriately."

"You're going on a date with Madison?" Hannah averted her eyes. "Oh, I see," she mumbled as she focused on her feet.

"Hannah?"

She didn't respond.

"Hannah? Is everything okay?"

She lifted her head and nodded. "Yep. Nope, all is well. In fact, I uh…I think that's wonderful news." Hannah exhaled. "See, I told you there was something between you two," she said in a less than enthusiastic tone.

"Payson," Jason yelled from his office.

"I will put a smile on my face the day I walk out of here and never have to deal with him anymore." She grabbed her notebook and headed to his office.

"Take a seat," he grumbled without looking up from his computer.

She did as she was told. "What's up?"

"Today, I want you…" He turned away from his computer and glanced at her. "What happened? Did someone die?"

"What?"

"You're all dressed up in black with makeup on and stuff. You going to a funeral?"

"Seriously Jason, that's where your mind went? No, I'm not going to a funeral. If you must know, I have a date later this evening."

He scoffed. "I don't need to know that. Why did you tell me that? As long as you have a good show tonight, I could give a shit what you do in your off hours."

"But you just asked if…never mind." She repositioned herself. "What's up?"

He flicked a piece of paper across his desk. "A couple of Elvis impersonators apparently got drunk last night and thought it would be funny to run around the neon boneyard with just their guitars on while singing "Hound Dog." A tourist claims to have caught the whole thing on his phone. See if you can get a copy of that video."

"I'll put Tegan on it."

"Oh, and the strippers on wheels caused an accident in the early morning hours after one of the pole dancers flipped upside down and spread her legs. The city's now talking about shutting it down. Put Patty on that story. I want it in the A-block."

She nodded as she scribbled in her notepad. The stunt to encase a flatbed trailer with Plexiglas, lit from within, and have pole dancers in lingerie do their thing in it while the truck slowly drove down Las Vegas Boulevard might have been a great marketing stunt for the strip clubs, but it created friction with the city council from day one. But controversy translated to free publicity, and in this town of extremes, anything a business could do to rise above the weird won them the game. "Sounds good. Anything else?"

"Give it five minutes, but for now, that's all I got. Oh, and don't forget the humane society's coming in with their puppies tonight."

"I know, I'm giving them three minutes in the B-block."

"Bump them to the bottom of the C-block, and cut their segment to two minutes. If the Elvis video pans out, give that more time."

"But you know the viewers love to see the puppies. Why do I have to cut their time?" she said with a bit of a bite because she was starting to become resentful of Jason always undermining her decisions.

"Because I like the naked Elvis story better." He waved a dismissive hand as he took a call.

Jason's wrong, she thought as she strolled back to her cubicle. The puppy segment was much more appealing than a bunch of drunk Elvises. That story might be good for a quick laugh, but this was Vegas; who wasn't drunk and doing stupid things all day long?

"Everything okay?" Hannah asked.

"Just the normal insanity of the—"

A scream stopped the newsroom in its tracks. Payson spun and looked behind her. Two legs were sticking up from behind Madison's desk.

"Holy shit," Payson said as she and several others rushed over to help. Madison was sitting in a chair that was lying on the floor, her hands gripped the arm rests, and her feet were straight up in the air. "Madison, are you okay?" She hooked her arm around Madison's shoulder and helped her up.

"That damn chair!" Madison snarled as she straightened her clothes and patted her hair. "Jason," she screamed. "I want my own office with brand-new furniture…now!" She stormed into the corner office and slammed the door.

"That's so weird," Payson muttered as she returned to her cubicle. "I know I put that chair in the corner yesterday with a sign that clearly said it was broken. I don't know how it ended up in Madison's cubicle."

"Huh…imagine that," was all Hannah said as she displayed a slight grin.

As the day progressed, Payson received several flirtatious texts from Madison, all alluding to her coming over for an after-dinner drink. At one point, she caught Madison wink at her as she walked past. But if a suggestive exchange was what Madison had in mind, it fell short of its mark. Because instead of returning the gesture, she choked back a chuckle as the image of Madison lying on the floor flashed in her head. The unexpected reaction caught her off guard. She was excited about the prospect of having a romantic evening with Madison, that was undeniable, so why the humorous reaction to an overtly suggestive signal? And not only that, there was something else that had her feeling a bit off, and it had nothing to do with Madison.

She began noticing it every time she was close to Hannah. There was a strange, almost magnetic pull that seemed to make her want to gravitate toward her. And each time they touched, a feeling of warm calmness surrounded her heart, as though it recognized Hannah in some familiar way. She had to admit, she had never felt that sensation with anyone before, and it was a bit unnerving.

She shook the thoughts from her mind as she tried to concentrate on writing the show's opening teaser. "Get it together," she mumbled to herself because as the day wore on, she was having a harder time figuring out which of them was causing her desires to be pinged in a way she hadn't felt in a long time. If ever.

Thirty minutes before the show was to begin, the police scanners began screeching. Payson jumped up, grabbed her notepad, and hustled to the assignment desk. Jason lumbered out of his office. "What's going on?"

"Sounds like a street performer and a tourist got into a fight on Fremont Street, and the end result was a stabbing."

"That's your lead." He called. "Pull Tegan away from the neon boneyard and get her over there now. I want her to be at the scene when the show opens. Come on, people, move."

Payson scurried back to her cubicle, notified Tegan of the change in plans, and reminded her to check in when she was set up and ready to go. This was the sprint before the show; stories needed to be shuffled around, reporters shifted, information gathered, and scripts written. She tilted her head from shoulder to shoulder as her neck cracked. She needed to focus and get in her zone. She let out a long breath as she stared at her computer and blocked out everything around her.

"Talk to me," she whispered to the screen, and a moment later, her fingers flew over her keyboard as words filled her mind.

As the countdown to the show neared, she started tapping her leg. She was ninety seconds over. "Damn," she mumbled. She still needed to cut, but she didn't want to take any more time away from the puppies, so she pulled a segment about an elderly woman who was going to do a charity swim in Lake Mead for her eightieth birthday and shelved it for tomorrow's show.

Fifteen minutes out, Payson hit the print icon. "Done," she announced as Hannah scurried to the printer and gathered the scripts. They hustled into the studio and placed two copies on the desk as Madison and her male co-anchor shuffled in, ready to deliver the tragic, bizarre, and strange to the viewers with a smile. The anchors settled into their designated positions and mic'd up as Hannah and Payson took their seats in the control room and threw their headsets on. Payson flipped buttons and called reporters to make sure everyone was in place and ready to go as the overhead clock ticked down the seconds. This was the adrenaline rush of the business, and it invigorated her as much as exhausted her.

"Get ready, Tegan. You're on in thirty," Payson told her over her phone.

"And…cue, Tegan," the director called, and a shot of Tegan standing on Fremont Street, surrounded by a crowd, filled the screen. The red and blue flashing police lights added to the overpowering neon and made for a picture that would definitely grab the attention of any viewer. Tegan spoke with concern on her face as she explained how a dispute over the price a street performer was charging a tourist for taking a selfie of the two of them had turned into an altercation that sent one person to the hospital in serious condition.

"And cue, package," Payson said after Tegan delivered her live monologue.

Tegan's story, peppered with interviews and eye-witness accounts, went live, and Payson let her know she would toss to her again in a minute and forty. The piece was not the most riveting, but it would get the locals talking about how the city needed to keep the street performers safe from drunken tourists. This was, after all, one of their own who was attacked.

"Get ready, Tegan," Payson told her. "You're back on in thirty. And heads-up, Madison said she's going to pitch a question or two to you, so be prepared for that. But I'll need you to wrap it up within a thirty-second window."

"Got it."

As stories unfolded, one after the other, Payson got into a synchronized motion. For thirty minutes every weeknight, this was her stage. This was the performance she had prepared all day for. She was the puppeteer behind the scenes, and how successful or not the show looked to the viewer was a direct result of her. It was as addicting as it was exhilarating, and it was why she stayed in a job that was slowly sucking the life out of her.

As the newscast began to wind down, so did her adrenaline. By the time she pitched to the puppy segment, she felt like she had run a marathon. She exhaled an accomplished breath. She was at the bottom of the C-block, the show was about to end, and she now had one more newscast under her belt. As the studio cameras shot closeups of the fuzzy faces of the latest puppies available for adoption at the local shelter, her heart melted. She thought of eighteen years of Kona kisses, and tears welled in her eyes. Kona had left much more than pawprints around Payson's house; she'd also left them all over her heart, and they became heavier with each passing day.

"And we're clear. Good show, people." The words of the director brought her back to reality.

"Yes," Payson added. "Good show, people." She pulled the headset off and glanced at Hannah. "Well, let's go out there and pet some puppies before Jason comes in and ruins the mood with his list of criticisms," she said as she stood and arched her back. Every now and then, the perks of the job outweighed the stress and made it all worthwhile. Being in a studio full of puppies every week was definitely top of that list.

"Payson." Hannah gently grasped her arm.

A shiver shot up her body, and her erect nipples made another appearance. "Yeah?"

"I just wanted to say that I hope you have a wonderful dinner tonight with Madison."

Payson glanced at Hannah's arm as a slight warmth infused her body. There were definitely moments in the day when she could have sworn that she and Hannah had chemistry. She would catch her from the corner of her eye, staring, or their hands would linger and not move after an accidental touch. But maybe she was wrong. Maybe she was just projecting her own feelings; after all, ever since Hannah had come to the station, she seemed more focused on getting Payson together with Madison then herself.

"Thank you," Payson muttered as she gazed at Hannah. She was beautifully sexy, seemed uncomplicated, and smiled with childlike wonder at almost everything. She seemed interested in Payson's life, marveled at the things Payson took for granted, and had an insightful way of explaining the world. "Well, uh…" Payson teetered a bit as she became lost in Hannah's eyes and contemplated leaning in and kissing her. But when Hannah broke eye contact and looked down, she shook her head in embarrassment. What was she doing? She had a date with Madison tonight, and here she was almost kissing Hannah. She rubbed her temples as she thought again about how strange the past twenty-four hours had been. With the sudden attention from Madison and the instant attraction toward Hannah hitting at the same time, maybe she was confusing her emotions. After all, it was clear that Madison was the one interested in her, not Hannah. But still, there was that gut feeling about Hannah that told her that there was something about her that connected them.

"Well," she said as she brushed the thoughts off. Whatever it is, she'll worry about it later. "I'll tell you all about it tomorrow."

"It's just that…" Hannah trailed off as she raised her head.

"It's just what?" *Say it.* Payson needed to know that what she had been feeling these past two days was mutual. She needed Hannah to tell her that she too could feel the spark between them. That her gut instinct was right. Even if she couldn't explain it, she just needed validation that she wasn't the only one feeling a little scared and unsure about the attraction. *Say it, Hannah.* She searched the faraway look in Hannah's eyes for a sign that said she wasn't imagining everything. That the pull she felt between them was real. But a blink later, Hannah once again averted her eyes and widened their distance.

"Nothing," Hannah mumbled. "I, um, I can't wait to hear all about it tomorrow."

"You guys coming?" The studio director peeked his head back in. "Jason's waiting."

Payson nodded. "Sure," she said in a dry tone. "We'll be right out. Come on." She cocked her head to Hannah. "Let's go hear what Jason thought about the show."

"I meant what I said, Payson. I really do hope the evening brings you everything you desire."

"Will you stop it?" Payson waved her off, a little annoyed. "I get it, you think Madison and I are made for each other and all that matchmaker stuff." She didn't mean to snap, but she was getting tired of the contradiction between what Hannah was signaling and what she was saying. "Now, come on. I don't want to talk about it anymore."

As they entered the studio, a dozen puppies were running around playing with crew members. She scooped one up and showered it with kisses as Brandon, the director of the humane society, approached. "Thanks again for giving us airtime. It always helps with the adoptions," he said.

"Well, I'd make it a daily part of the show if I could. Anything to help these guys find a forever home." Her eyes drifted to one puppy shaking and cowering in the corner. "Is that one okay?" she asked with a tilt of her head.

"That's little Tucker. We just got him in a couple of days ago. He came from a pretty nasty case of abuse, and I was hoping we could showcase him tonight, but I think the little guy needs more time to build up his trust."

"Hmm." Hannah stepped around Payson and approached the puppy. He cowered when she sat and extended her hand.

Madison sauntered over. "Ready to…oh my God, that dog is slobbering all over your dress."

Payson looked down at a little wet spot spreading across her chest and chuckled. "That's okay." She lifted the chubby furball and buried her face in his. "It's all good, huh, big boy?"

"Think it's time to get another one?" Brandon asked.

Payson shook her head. "My heart says yes, but my reality says no. But as soon as that changes, I'll let you know," she said as she handed him the puppy.

Madison huffed. "We really need to get going. And please do something about that wet spot on your dress. It looks like you're lactating."

Payson glanced at her chest and smiled. She didn't care about the wetness; it was worth it to snuggle with a little one and once again be the recipient of such unconditional love. "Don't worry, it'll be dry by the time I get to the restaurant." She brushed at the spot.

"I hope so. I really don't want to be embarrassed. This is a five-star restaurant, you know. Now, come on, we really need to get going. I pulled some strings to get this reservation, and I don't want to be late," she said as she hooked her arm around Payson and led her away.

Payson stopped walking and turned. "Let me just say good-bye to Hannah."

"Don't worry about the temp. We need to get going…now."

"Her name's Hannah." And as though Hannah heard, she turned and glanced at Payson. There was something in her eyes, as though she was either pleading or in some way saying her good-byes. Payson took a step in her direction as the pull between them resurfaced.

A hand landed with a thud on her shoulder. "Whatever," Madison snapped. "Look, our reservation is in an hour. By the time we valet and walk the casino, we should have left ten minutes ago."

Payson refocused on her. "Um." She shook her head and cleared her thoughts. "Yeah, okay, let's go." But as they were leaving, she glanced over her shoulder one last time and saw Hannah mouth the word, "Bye."

Payson and Madison gathered their belongings from their cubicles and split up as they approached their cars. "Last one there buys the first glass of wine," Madison called as she hopped in her car and sped out of the lot.

"Why am I always buying the drinks?" Payson said to no one as she opened her car door. Her gut churned, and the hair on the back of her neck stook on end as an internal voice told her to turn. She twisted her upper body and stared at the station's back door as it swung open.

"Hannah?" she called as goose bumps tingled her skin, and the strange pull once again surfaced, but it was just Brandon getting something from his van. She shook her head and chuckled as she melted into her car, a bit perplexed. What the hell was going on with her?

"Stop thinking about Hannah," she mumbled as she threw her car in drive. It was a beautiful night, she was having dinner at an amazing restaurant, and if she and Madison clicked, then it was clear how the evening would end. But as she pulled up to the casino's valet, something was still nagging at her that she couldn't quite identify or bring into focus. As though she were trying to make out a distant figure in a thick fog.

"Hey," Madison said as she stood waiting outside the restaurant. She flipped her hair off her shoulder and displayed her signature grin.

Madison was society's definition of gorgeous. She checked all the boxes: flawless skin, thin, long hair, bright eyes, and a big flirtatious smile. *Which is exactly why Jason hired her.* As long as she could read a teleprompter and look damn good doing it, that was all he cared about. Even in the world of delivering facts and figures to the general public, a woman still had to do it while looking "fuckable." And Madison definitely delivered on all counts.

And there was a part of Payson's ego that got a boost from being here with her tonight. But as she approached Madison, her mind drifted again to Hannah, and she snorted. Hannah would never be hired as a news anchor because, according to the standards of the business, she didn't possess the definition of the "it" factor. Yet, between the two, Payson definitely thought Hannah was more "fuckable." She smiled at that thought as she lowered her head and approached Madison.

"I meant to tell you this earlier. You look nice," Madison said.

Nice was not quite as complimentary as when Hannah had said she looked stunning, but she'd take it. "Thank you." She tucked a strand of her hair behind her ear as she felt a slight heat flush her face. She still didn't understand what had sparked the sudden attention from Madison, but she had to admit, it was quite flattering.

"Are you hungry?" Madison asked through her signature smile.

"Are you kidding? I'm starving. I purposely didn't eat this afternoon so I could savor every bite from this place." She had been on the restaurant's website a half dozen times today, drooling over photographs of the award-winning dishes the Michelin chef created. If the food tasted half as good as the pictures looked, Payson was in for one hell of a treat.

As they approached the hostess, Madison dropped her name, and they were escorted to the lower section of the restaurant where the tables had a perfect view of the strip. Payson could feel the eyes of some of the patrons watch them walk by, and although she was feeling sexy this evening, she knew the eyes weren't on her. Madison could command the attention of any room she walked in, and Payson could tell by the shift in her strut that she was well-aware of her captive audience. This was her stage as much as the studio was, and Payson understood that. But she wondered, if she and Madison did hook up, would living in that shadow ever be enough to satisfy her?

They settled into their seats, and Payson glanced out the window. The view of the strip was spectacular. No matter how tired she'd grown of Vegas, she couldn't help but get caught up in its energy as the town came alive at night. People packed the streets, water danced to music in lagoons, and every color imaginable flashed and flickered in a neon display. This was the artificial dance of the city, and she had to admit, it was mesmerizing.

A man in a chef's outfit appeared. "Madison, you look magnificent as ever."

"Antoine, darling, how are you?" Madison stood, gave him a hug, then turned. "Antoine, Payson. Payson, Antoine."

He extended his hand. "Nice to meet you. The view from here is incredible, no?"

"Magical. Simply magical," Payson said as she glanced again at the strip.

"I owe you one, buddy," Madison said.

He waved her off. "You owe me nothing. But…if you want to MC a charity event my wife is hosting next month, I would be forever grateful."

Madison threw her head back in animated laughter. "Leave the information, and I'll think about it. Now, what's good?"

"The truffle ravioli with deep fried pureed artichoke and the seared scallops in green curry with young leeks are exquisite tonight."

"Perfect, we'll have the scallops. And two glasses of Chenin Blanc."

Payson pursed her lips tightly together and cocked her head as she thought about all the times her ex had ordered for her when they went out to eat and how much that annoyed her. It wasn't that the scallops wouldn't be exceptional, but of the two choices, she would rather have had the ravioli. And as for the wine, she was definitely not a connoisseur or well-versed in pairings, but she knew what she liked, and she liked a good pinot noir. And the fact that Madison didn't bother to even ask soured her stomach. But instead of speaking up, she remained silent and nodded her approval. Hmm, maybe she hadn't made as many post-breakup gains as she'd thought, since she so quickly fell back into old submissive habits.

"Excellent, now, I shall leave you two beautiful ladies alone to enjoy your evening while I go prepare your food. I'll let your server know your order. Bon Appetit."

"How do you two know each other?" Payson asked after he walked away.

"Antoine? We go way back. He used to own a small restaurant in Chicago where my sister worked as a server. I ate there a lot, and we became fast friends."

"I never knew you had a sister."

Madison nodded. "And a brother, but we're not a very close family. When I was a kid, we all used to..."

And just like Sam, Madison whisked Payson down memory lane. And by the time she drank her wine and finished her meal, she was still listening to Madison talk about her career, her aspirations, and her accomplishments. When dessert arrived, the story of her life had only advanced to her mid-twenties.

Although the conversation was completely one-sided, she gave Madison credit. The woman was gifted in making every story completely compelling, and it was nice to finally have a broader, more intimate picture of her, and it explained a bit more why she was who she was. And as the night lingered and Madison showed a more vulnerable side, Payson's opinion of her softened. Still, there were moments when her mind floated to Hannah, and she wondered what she was doing. If she had gone out for drinks with everyone or if she was settled in for the evening in her hotel room.

As Payson finished the last bite of dessert, her mind started to drift to whether she and Madison were really meant for each other, as Hannah had said. She focused on Madison's fingers wrapping around the wineglass, and wondered what those fingers would feel like as they explored her inside and out. But as her body began reacting to that thought, and she felt a heat emerge between her legs, that strong gut feeling reemerged, and Madison morphed once again into Hannah. And it was Hannah's fingers scratching the itch that had been building in her all day. She glanced out the window and again wondered what Hannah was doing tonight.

CHAPTER NINE

Hannah waved good-bye as she watched Madison turn Payson around and escort her out of the studio. She fought the urge to chase her down and tell her not to go out with Madison but instead have dinner with her. But she backed off and reminded herself that if she and Payson were meant to be together, Payson would choose to come to her.

"Oh well," she mumbled as tears welled in her eyes. "We'll know soon enough." Tucker jumped up and began licking the wet from her face. She chuckled as she bent, picked him up, and held him close.

"I can't believe what I'm seeing. He hasn't responded like that to any of our staff," Brandon said as he approached.

"I'll take him." The words flew out of her mouth as she looked into Tucker's big brown eyes. She had been told that the eyes always held the unspoken words of the soul, and what was fear and distrust now became hope in his. She would forever be haunted with worry over his future and well-being if she did not bring him back to the island with her. "You are the second pair of eyes that I've fallen for," she whispered as she kissed his head.

"Wonderful. Can you swing by the shelter tomorrow morning? We can do the paperwork, then."

"No, I'm sorry. I won't be around tomorrow. I'll probably be leaving town tonight."

He scrubbed his chin. "Well, I do have a few forms in the van. Let me go get them. Can you pay cash, or should I write down your credit card number?"

"I have cash." Hannah reached in her pockets and pulled out everything she had. "Here, take it all." She held a couple bills back and handed him the rest.

He fanned through the money. "That's very generous of you. Let me get the form." As he walked out the back door, she once again thought about Payson's date with Madison.

"Don't chase her," she reminded herself, even though the thought of anyone else's hands touching Payson's body sent a surge of jealousy through her veins. "She'll make her choice." And so Hannah stayed rooted in her spot, holding Tucker close and reminding herself that if she hadn't missed with her arrow in the first place, Payson and Madison would surely be united by now. All she had done was prolong the inevitable, and it was time to remove herself from a picture she should have never been in.

"Here you go," Brandon said as he presented her with the forms and a bag of essentials.

Maybe, she thought as she filled out the paperwork with bogus information, she was meant to come here not for Payson but for Tucker. To rescue a soul who needed love in the worst way. Yes, she concluded as she thanked him, scooped Tucker up, and walked out the door, love was meant for all living souls.

"Come on, little one, it's time to go home," she said as she walked away from the station. She didn't need to gather anything from her desk nor give the newsroom a parting glance. She would not miss this place or look back upon it fondly. But she did take one last hopeful glance around the lot to see if

Payson had chosen to stay and not go on the dinner date. But the empty lot confirmed what she already knew.

"Maybe I should have chased her down after all, huh, Tucker?" she said as her chest tightened, and her stomach bottomed out. She would have bet a quiver of golden arrows that she and Payson were the would-be lovers who were destined for each other. She chuckled at the thought; so much for the natural instinct Oriana had always told her she possessed. Maybe the takeaway lesson in all of this was a repeat of the same lesson the wind had taught her as a child. *Listen more and don't be so stubborn in your own beliefs.* The universe, Danika, Piper, and Oriana had all told her what she didn't want to hear. What she'd refused to listen to. And now, she only had herself to blame. Life's lessons could sure suck.

Tucker squirmed a bit in her arms, interrupting her thoughts, so she placed him on the ground and loosely held his leash. "Piper will be here soon to take us home. You're going to love it on the island. It's everything I promised you." She set a slow pace as the two of them shuffled in the direction Gimbauld's. She continued to tell him stories of Bella and the lake, of the cottage they would share, and the fields he could run free in. And the more she talked, the more she realized the distraction was a great way to tamp down the numbness that was rapidly taking hold as she continued to think about Payson.

When they reached their destination, she scooped up Tucker and walked through the casino. As she entered her room, she retrieved two bowls from the bag Brandon had given her, placed food and water in them, and sat on the floor next to him. She leaned against the bed, put her head back, and waited for Piper to appear. Her time was up, she had Tucker, and she had done what she was sent to do. There was at least some satisfaction in that.

She didn't know how long she had been asleep when the softest of knocks woke her, so quiet, she had to concentrate to make sure the sound was coming from her own door. "Piper?" she said in a groggy voice as she stood. "Why are you knocking?" She reached for the doorknob. "Why didn't you just teleport into the—" The next sound that made it to her lips was a breath. Or lack thereof. There, on the other side of the door, stood Payson in all her beauty. "What are you doing here? I… um…I don't understand. Why aren't you with Madison?"

"I was with Madison. But I was just…" Payson trailed off as she gazed at Hannah. "I just," she repeated, as she took a step toward her and leaned in. Hannah could smell the freshness of the night air still lingering on Payson's clothes and the hint of lavender mixed into her perfume. Both were intoxicating, and as Hannah closed her eyes and anticipated the kiss she…wait… the kiss!

Hannah's eyes popped open, and she took a couple steps back as unanswered questioned logjammed in her mind.

"Wow, I…um," Payson mumbled as she began backing away. "I'm sorry, I don't know what I was thinking. It's just…" She trailed off. "It's just that I have had the strangest couple of days, but, um, it's obvious I disturbed you and that this was just one big—"

"No," Hannah called out as she reached for her. "Please don't go. Stay…please." With a slight tilt of her head, she motioned for Payson to come in.

Payson hesitated, then nodded and entered. "Hey, you adopted Tucker." She bent on one knee, and Tucker wagged his tail, lowered his posture, and approached. He rolled over, and Payson scratched his belly as she cooed at him. "Oh no, he's peeing." She chuckled as Tucker squirted all over her hand.

Hannah hurried into the bathroom and emerged with two towels soaked in warm water. She gently rubbed one over his belly and the other over Payson's fingers. "How did you find me?"

"I know the woman who works at the front desk. She gave me your room number. I know that wasn't totally ethical, so I hope it's okay?"

"It is, but I'm still confused. Haven't you and Madison… um, you know…kissed yet?" Hannah's head was spinning as she tried to keep up with the reality of the situation. Since Payson was standing before her and not Piper, that meant either they'd kissed and the binding spell had failed, or…

She let out a breath, and her stomach tightened and tingled. Her instincts might have been right all along.

"I wish you would stop trying to push me and Madison together. And yes, we did almost kiss."

"Almost?"

Payson nodded. "The evening went well, the dinner was wonderful, and she asked me to follow her to her house for a drink. While we were waiting for the valet to get our cars, she leaned in to kiss me. Our lips were so close, I could feel her breath. But then, I don't know…something weird happened," she said in a faraway voice. "Just before our lips touched, a gust of wind blew my hair in my face. When I pulled the hair out of my eyes, I just stood there staring at her. She was looking back at me as though she was waiting for me to finish what she'd started. But…all I could see at that moment was you." She ran a finger over Hannah's cheek. "This beautiful gorgeous face, and I just"—she licked her lips—"I just knew this is where I wanted to be. Where I *needed* to be."

Hannah placed a hand over Payson's. She felt the softness of her skin as she turned her hand and kissed her palm, and she knew in that moment that she would be forever lost if their lips touched. She let out a frustrated breath as she became consumed by desire. Her head spun, and she shivered as the chill of anticipation tickled up her body. She wanted to explore every inch of Payson. To lick, suck, and penetrate all of her. She leaned back and studied the eyes that mesmerized her and searched for a truth that lay beyond the reading of the night sky. She searched for Payson's truth. "Payson, I need to know something from you."

"Anything," Payson said as she closed the distance between them.

"I need to know you're absolutely sure that in your heart of hearts, this is really what you want. That *I'm* what you want," she whispered in Payson's ear as she brushed her cheek ever so softly against hers.

"From the moment I saw you, a feeling came over me that I haven't been able to shake. It's like…a gut feeling that keeps telling me we're meant to be together." She waved a hand in front of her face. "I know that sounds crazy and all, but I just can't get you out of my mind."

"As though," Hannah said as she took a step closer. "It was our names that were written in the stars." She took the moment to study her face.

Payson smiled back as she raised one hand and wrapped it behind Hannah's neck and began bringing her closer. Every inch of Hannah's body felt like it was going to explode. The desire to be touched was overwhelming her better judgment. "Are you sure you want me and no one else?" she whispered as Payson closed the gap between them.

"I'm surer of this than anything I've ever been sure of. Now, kiss me," Payson said as she let her lips linger on Hannah's.

For a moment, Hannah wondered if that was enough to summon Piper and teleport her back. But when Piper didn't appear, she kissed Payson deeply.

Payson let loose a breathy moan, that universal sound that said the other person not only enjoyed what they were receiving, but that they wanted so much more. Hannah slowly walked Payson backward to the bed and lowered her down. Hannah crawled on top and straddled her. Usually, when she started the act of lovemaking, she didn't come up for air until the end. But for the first time ever, she was filled with both desire and contentment. She wanted to make love to Payson as much as she wanted to hold her and talk endlessly about everything and nothing. "Payson, I…" She trailed off as she took a moment to stare at Payson and appreciate the beautiful butterfly that in the end, chose to come to her.

Payson placed a finger on Hannah's lips. "All I want to hear from you right now is the sound you make when you come."

Hannah's body flushed with heat, and she unbuttoned her shirt and tossed it on the floor. Her breath caught as Payson traced over her stomach muscles and up to her breasts. Payson squeezed her nipples, causing her to close her eyes and arch her back. Wetness released between her legs, and her pants seemed that much more restrictive. She rolled to Payson's side, shrugged out of them, then wrapped her fingers around the hem of Payson's dress and began pulling it over her body. With every inch of skin that the fabric revealed, Hannah's butterflies took another lap around her stomach. She positioned herself back over Payson and lowered her hips until she felt Payson's hair tickle her own. It sent a chill up her, and she paused a moment to enjoy the sensation before she pressed down and began a gentle grinding.

"Kiss me. Now," Payson whispered in one long moan.

Hannah gladly obeyed, and this time, as she kissed Payson deeply, her mind cleared of the consequences. She no longer concerned herself with whether or not she was cheating the universe or what Danika had or had not seen in the night sky. Payson wanted her, and she wanted Payson, and if there was an ounce of truth to the myths of love at first sight, then she was living it.

Payson broke the kiss and moved her lips to Hannah's ear. "Take me," was all she said, and Hannah felt each word cause a small spasm in her clit. She kneeled between Payson's legs as she caressed her breasts. They're so perfect, she thought as she bent, licked and sucked each erect nipple, then trailed her right-hand down Payson's abdomen. She used Payson's own wetness to tease her and slid the tips of her fingers in, out, and around her until she could sense Payson was ready for what she wanted to give.

Hannah bunched her first three fingers together and slid them inside. "Is this okay?" she asked as she maintained a slow pace until she was sure Payson was comfortable.

Payson responded by pressing her body more deeply onto Hannah's fingers and moving her hips at an accelerated rate. Hannah matched the pace, letting her fingers explore inside Payson's body. With her other hand, she caressed and pinched one of Payson's nipples.

"Yes, baby," Hannah whispered as a layer of sweat formed on her skin. She was completely turned on, and every time she thrust deeper, she almost came herself. But this wasn't about her, at least not yet. This was about pleasing Payson, so she blocked her own desires as she concentrated and listened to the way Payson's body was talking to her. How her hands gripped the sheets, the pace of her breath, and the extra wetness released around Hannah's fingers. And when Payson's thighs tightened and held, she knew what would soon follow.

Hannah increased her pace, and when she finally felt the throbbing around her fingers and Payson's body went from tense to relaxed, she slowed and gently slid her fingers out.

Payson's breath caught. Hannah placed the palm of her hand on the outside of Payson's clit and maintained pressure until a smile spread across Payson's face, and her eyes slowly peeled open.

Hannah returned the smile and once again straddled her. Payson cupped her face. Hannah began kissing the palm of Payson's hand, and when she reached her fingers, she licked them into her mouth and slowly began sucking. Payson raised a knowing brow as she slid her fingers from Hannah's mouth down her body. When she felt Payson's fingers slowly enter her, she moaned and shivered. She was so overstimulated that her body was on the verge of coming sooner than she wanted. But tonight marked the first night of their lovemaking, and like most *firsts*, Hannah wanted to savor every moment.

Payson sat up, wrapped her other arm around Hannah's lower back, and thrust her fingers deeper inside. When Hannah felt the sensation of Payson's thumb up and down her wetness and the soft whisper of her voice tickled her ear with the words, "Come for me, baby," Hannah gave in to the pleasure. The explosion that followed shook her to her core. With the fingers still in her, she hugged Payson tight until her heartbeat and breathing slowed to normal. Tonight had opened a Pandora's box of emotions that would be impossible to gather and put back. She wondered if this was what the recipients of her arrows felt when they got together; it was definitely an emotion she had never felt before.

She leaned back as Payson pulled her fingers out, and they fell back on the bed, side by side. She wrapped Payson in a gentle embrace. "You are the most beautiful woman I've ever known."

Payson lifted up on her elbow and stared. "I can't even remember the last time someone called me beautiful."

"Come here," she said as she brought her into a tight hug. "I promise to tell you every day how beautiful you are." She massaged Payson's hair as Payson rested her head on her chest. Hannah stared into space, wondering what she had done as she sensed Payson's breathing change into the soft slow rhythm of sleep. She had cheated the universe tonight, and she had no idea what that meant, what consequences would befall her, or what the future would hold. The only thing she knew for certain was that she could never bring Payson to the island because of the law. She closed her eyes as tears trickled down her cheeks. She softly kissed Payson's forehead, then nuzzled her cheek. Hannah's heart felt equal parts full of love and empty with sadness. To pursue a life with Payson meant she might have to say good-bye to everything she had ever known. And that daunting reality robbed her of any hope she had for a restful night's sleep.

❖

The thumping of a tiny tail against the side of the bed made Hannah smile. She carefully slid out from under Payson, and as her feet touched the carpet, a slobbery tongue began licking them. She scooped Tucker up, brought him in for morning kisses, carried him over to a pee pad, and dumped another handful of morsels in his bowl. She scrubbed his head, told him she loved him, then walked to the window. The city in daylight was not the same as at night. With the artificial colors of neon replaced by natural light, a very different and lackluster image of the strip emerged. Nowhere near as glamorous or glitzy and a far cry from her beloved island.

"Morning," Hannah said in a soft voice as warm hands wrapped around her waist.

"It looks like it's going to be a nice day," Payson said as she rested her chin on Hannah's shoulder.

Hannah pulled her into a deep kiss.

"Mmm, I could get use to waking up to this," Payson mumbled.

Hannah answered by kissing her again, then walking her backward to the bed and lowering her. "You could get used to this, huh?" She kissed the words down Payson's neck.

"Mm-hmm."

Hannah gently caressed her breast. "How about this? Could you get used to this?"

Payson let out a gasp as she bit her lip. "Oh, I definitely could get use to that."

Hannah kissed her stomach. "And this? How about this?"

Payson arched her back, and her fingers scrunched in Hannah's hair as she guided her down even farther. No more questions were asked or answers given. All the communicating that needed to happen from that point forward would be done with silent lips and exploring tongues.

An hour later, Hannah escorted Payson to the door as Piper appeared, startling her. She was leaning against the wall with Hannah's golden cuffs dangling from the fingers of one hand, and Hannah could tell from the magical sheen covering her skin that Piper was invisible to Payson.

"You okay?" Payson asked as she placed her hand on Hannah's shoulders and squeezed.

"Yeah." She faced Payson. "I'm fine. I just, um, I thought I heard something."

"We gotta go. Now," Piper said in a firm voice.

Hannah shooed Piper with her hand as she leaned in and kissed Payson. When they broke the embrace, they locked eyes. "I won't be at the station today. I'm afraid something's come up. But I will be in the parking lot waiting for you when you get off. I was thinking maybe we can do a late dinner and—"

"How about we forgo the food, and you come over to my place for a drink?" Payson smiled seductively.

Hannah raised a brow. "Even better."

"Then I guess I'll see you later?" Payson twiddled her fingers over her shoulder as she strolled down the hall. Hannah leaned against the door frame and watched Payson disappear toward the elevators.

"She's beautiful," Piper said as she craned her neck past Hannah. "I hope she was worth it."

"More than worth it," Hannah replied. Payson was everything she found endearing, and she was perfect in every way. Hannah turned to face Piper as dread churned in her stomach. "I've been expecting you. In fact, I figured you'd come for me last night," she said as they settled back into the room.

"I did." Piper smiled. "I was sent to bring you back right after you two kissed and ended the binding spell, but I didn't have the heart to interrupt."

"So you saw?"

"I saw enough, yes."

"And yet you didn't take me away?"

"Why should I? At that point, the spell had already been broken. I figured there was no harm in letting you two have your fun. Besides, it gave me time to play another night of cards."

Hannah frowned. "Oriana will not be pleased with either of us."

"No, she won't. But that's nothing new. Now come on, we really need to go." Piper handed Hannah her cuffs. "Ready?"

The moment Hannah was reunited with her bracers, she let out a content breath. She quickly clasped them on and took a moment to be reminded of what they represented to her.

"Ready," she replied with a nod as she scooped up Tucker. And as with the news station, she didn't feel the need to take one last lingering look around the room. But as she glanced at the bed, where the tangled covers still showed evidence of their lovemaking, she knew going home would be bittersweet. In the eyes of Oriana, she had failed in her mission, but to Hannah, she had found the one thing she had been searching for her whole life. But was it worth the exile she might be facing upon her return? Knowing that she might be spending the rest of her life living amongst the mortals if she pursued anything with Payson? She didn't have an answer, but as she glanced again at the bed, she knew she had never felt so completely alive in her life until now.

Chapter Ten

Payson entered the bakery with a bit of a bounce in her step. As the bells on the door jingled, Sam looked up. "Payson!" He held up his finger, signaling for her to wait. He grabbed a waxed paper with muffin pieces cut in squares on it. He placed the paper on the counter and with a big grin said, "My daughter's newest flavor, what do you think?"

Payson took a fingerful of crumbled pastry and placed it in her mouth as he leaned in with wide expectant eyes and a huge, *I already know what you're going to say*, grin. He raised a brow. "So?"

Payson swallowed the mouthful of goodness and nodded. "That tastes amazing. Sam, it's so delicious."

"My daughter has the gift, yes?" His smile reflected the pride that Payson was sure he was feeling.

"Yes. She definitely has the gift." She scooped up another fingerful of crumbs and shoved them in her mouth.

"She keeps telling me that we need to think about expanding the reach of the bakery. She's been trying to get appointments at the casinos. To either use us as a supplier for their pastries or talk to them about renting some space for our own sales. But you know how it is." He waved a dismissive hand. "Without contacts, it's hard to get in to see anyone."

"I do know how that is. Let me see if I can make some calls and at least try to set her up to see someone. I think she may be on to something."

"She reminds me of her mother. In fact, did I ever tell you about the time…" And with those words wrapping around her, she was escorted on another scenic stroll down memory lane. She nodded, smiled and pointed to select baked goods, barely listening to what he was saying because as he replayed the memories of his wife, she replayed the highlights of last night's lovemaking. She thought about the way Hannah's body felt while pressed against hers and the way her tongue skillfully moved deep in her mouth.

"Payson?"

She blinked back in her surroundings and noticed Sam staring at her. "I'm sorry, what?"

"I asked if this was all for today?" He motioned to the bag.

"Yes, that will be all. Thank you so much, and please tell Amanda I think she's a baking goddess."

"A baking goddess." He chuckled. "She'll like that one."

She handed over her money and as per usual, placed the change in the tip jar. She grabbed the bag, thanked him again, and headed for the door. "She *is* a baking goddess, and you'll see. Her vision will pay off one of these days. I have a good feeling about it." She pushed through the door. "See you tomorrow, Sam, and have a wonderful day."

"You too, Payson," he called back.

As she scurried across the parking lot, a strange feeling tickled the back of her neck, as though someone was watching her. She stopped and glanced around. Nothing. Then she shielded her eyes and squinted toward the rooftop. In her mind, she could see the image of Hannah sitting with a bow and arrow in hand, staring at her. She smiled at the thought. "As crazy as it seems, my gut says that really was you," she muttered to no one, then turned and headed into the building. But why in the world would someone sent from corporate be on a rooftop with a weapon, dressed in a costume?

Tegan hopped on Payson's desk. "Wow, don't you look all happy and glowing? I'm assuming the date with Madison went well?"

"The date with Madison did go well, but that's not why I'm smiling." She handed over the bag. "Take what you want, I bought extra."

"Don't tell me Jason finally approved your vacation time?" Tegan said as she shuffled through the contents of the bag, pulled out a muffin, and took a bite.

"Nope." Hannah grabbed a scone and sat in her chair.

"Okay, first of all, these are the best muffins I've ever had. Amanda's rocking it in the bakery."

"I know. Sam told me she has a vision to expand their business."

"They should." Tegan took another bite. "These are awesome," she mumbled as she nodded. "Okay, back to you. What's with the pregnant glow and goofy grin?"

"Well." Payson rolled her chair a little closer. "After I saw Madison last night, I ended up going to see Hannah in her hotel room, and we kinda…"

"Shut the fuck up. You guys got together?"

"Shh." Payson giggled. "Not so loud, and yes, we got together." Payson felt the warmth of heat flash across her face.

"Well about time you got laid. How was it?"

"It was wonderful, amazing, and incredible." Hannah had a softness that completely contradicted her masculine side. And yet, when Payson had signaled that she wanted it a little rougher, Hannah knew exactly how far to take it.

"Huh, if I didn't know any better, I'd say you, my friend, are smitten. Damn, girl, I'm so happy for you."

"Thanks, I'm happy too. Which is why I know this is going to sound weird, but I need a favor," Payson said in a low voice.

"Okay." Tegan bent forward. "What's up?"

"Can you make some calls and run a background check on Hannah?"

Tegan cocked her head. "On Hannah?" She leaned back. "What's this about?"

"I just want to be a hundred percent sure about her before I fall any harder."

"Hannah isn't Julie," Tegan said in a, *why are you doing this*, kind of tone.

"I know that, I just…it's just…" She lowered her voice. "I'm seeing her later tonight, and if it's anything like last night, by tomorrow morning, I'll be in too deep to turn around."

"Is she not coming in today?" Tegan asked.

"No, something came up, which is why we're seeing each other later."

"You sure you want me to do this? If she ever finds out you requested a background check, it could be a bit awkward."

"She's not going to find out. Besides, I'm sure everything will be fine, and you won't find any red flags. Just say you'll do it so I can put my mind at ease."

"Of course I'll do it. But for the record"—She hopped off Payson's desk—"I don't feel comfortable running it on Hannah. I like her. My gut says she's a good person."

"So does mine, but I want to make sure I don't make another mistake. I think I could really fall for her."

"As if you haven't already."

"I owe you dinner."

"I'm going to take you up on that." Tegan waved a finger.

"I'm counting on it."

"Okay, give me everything you have on her. Last name, age, where she works, cell number." Tegan grabbed a pen and paper off Payson's desk.

Payson paused when she realized how little she really knew. "Her last name's um…uh, I actually don't know her last name." A twinge of anxiety was triggered as she thought about her ex and how little she really knew about her. About all the times Julie had sidestepped and changed conversations dealing with parts of her past. "Corporate sent her, so they'll have it, and she's staying at Gimbauld's in room 623, so they'll probably have info on her as well. And oh." she snapped her fingers. "She also does some work for an online dating service, but I'm not sure which one. Their motto has something to do with guaranteeing the clients fall in love."

Tegan frowned. "Please tell me you at least exchanged numbers."

She shook her head. "We, uh, we never did." Come to think of it, she couldn't remember seeing Hannah with a phone. Goose bumps formed on her skin as an uneasy feeling gripped her, but just as quickly, she shook it off as ridiculous paranoia. "Oh, wait a second. She adopted Tucker after last night's puppy segment, so I'm sure Brandon had her fill out some forms."

"Okay, give me a few hours, and I'll see what I can find."

Payson waved her off as she sat in silent thought. She was falling for someone she had only known a few short days, and it was apparent the word *known* was loosely defined. So much for her promise to *really get to know someone* before jumping headfirst into another relationship. She thought about the saying that lightning never strikes twice as she tried to dismiss her growing concerns. Even so, she would have to remember to get a little more information from Hannah when she saw her tonight.

"Payson," Jason called from his office.

She rolled her eyes as she grabbed her notepad. She glanced again at Hannah's empty cubicle as a surge of anticipation for the night shot through her. Even Jason couldn't dampen her mood today. Although, she thought as she shuffled to his office, the day was still young.

❖

Several hours later, Payson was touching up a promotional plug for the annual celebrity charity poker tournament that the station sponsored when Tegan dropped a manilla folder on her desk, startling her. "What's this?" Payson reached for the folder.

Tegan slapped a hand on it. "It's Hannah's background check, and I suggest you open this after the show tonight."

"What? Why?" She slowly pulled the folder out from under Tegan's hand.

"Payson…"

"Oh, stop being so dramatic. How bad could it be?" she said as she opened the folder, pulled out a piece of paper, scanned it, then flipped it over. "I don't understand. There's nothing here." She tilted her head toward Tegan. "Every category is blank."

"Exactly. Seems we have a bit of a mystery on our hands. Hannah is a ghost."

"A ghost?" The word struck her face like a slap. It was the exact word Tegan had used to describe Julie after she'd asked Tegan to track her down.

"She doesn't exist." Tegan continued. "She listed her last name as Archer, and the address Gimbauld's has on file for her isn't a real one. But as we know, giving a fake name and addresses to a hotel isn't unusual for this town, based on some of the clientele that come here and wish to remain anonymous." Tegan paused. "Should I continue?"

Payson heard the words through a thick fog forming around her brain as she barely nodded.

"Her room was prepaid in cash for three days only, so there's no credit card information there…oh, and she has already checked out. I also couldn't find a driver's license, birth certificate, email, or social security number that links to her. No criminal record, which is good, but also nothing when I did a job history search. And get this, I called a contact over at corporate, and she said she didn't know anything about an experimental temp project. She said they wouldn't do that sort of thing."

"Wait," Payson said as each word pounded in her head. "Back up. Jason said he talked to someone at corporate who set her up as my temp."

Tegan shook her head. "He talked to *someone*...but not someone at corporate."

Payson sank deep into her chair. Her mind volleyed between disbelief and numbness. "But that makes no sense. Why would anyone fake being a temp?" And why a temp assigned to her?

"I don't know, but all I'm saying is that when someone uses false names and addresses, there's a reason...and usually that reason is never a good one."

The walls began to spin, and Payson's stomach bottomed out as she doubled over in her chair. "I think I'm going to be sick."

Tegan's caring hand gently squeezed her shoulder. "Sorry, Payson, I know you were into her. And hell, I liked her too."

Her face flushed with heat. Did she really fall for another drifter? A con artist who wasn't who she said she was? When she could no longer breathe through the suffocating feeling, she bolted out of her chair and ran to the bathroom. She crashed through a stall door and bent over the toilet. She placed her hands on her thighs as the saliva in her mouth started to build. She spit a few times, but nothing more came up.

After a few minutes, she leaned against the stall door, took a few shaky breaths, then walked to the sink. She dampened a paper towel with cold water and ran it over her forehead. She felt like she had been duped once again. She glanced in the mirror as she studied the face reflected back. What was it about her that seemed to attract these types of women? Or was it this town? Vegas was a double-edged sword. The glamor and glitz designed to lure with hopes and dreams of striking it rich also attracted the desperate and dishonest.

The squeak of the bathroom door made her turn.

"You okay?" Tegan asked.

"Mm-hmm," she lied as she tossed the wet towel in the trash and leaned against the counter. Was she okay? No, not even close.

"I need to head over to the welcome sign for the mayor's speech, but I don't want to leave you like this," Tegan said as she approached.

Payson waved her off as she wiped tears from her cheek. "I'm okay, really."

"You don't look okay."

Payson pushed off the counter. "I'm fine, really. Now, go on. Jason will have your head if you miss that press conference." She turned and checked herself in the mirror as she fidgeted with her shirt. Her eyes were puffy, and her skin looked oxygen deprived, but it wasn't like anyone would notice. They were an hour out from the show, so everyone would be in scramble mode. "Come on. We both have a job to do."

Tegan pulled her into a tight hug. "I'm so sorry, sweetie. I really thought she was the real thing too."

"Well." Payson pulled out of the hug as a fresh tear escaped. "At least it was short-lived, and she didn't clean out my bank account." She smiled, even though her heart was breaking.

"Yeah, I guess there's that," Tegan said. "But I'm still gonna worry about you."

"I'll be fine. I've worked my way out of disappointment and heartache before." She waved her hand. "Now go, be the amazing reporter that you are."

Tegan laughed as they shuffled back into the newsroom. "You might want to remind Jason of that from time to time. I could use a raise."

"You and me both," Payson said as she returned to her cubicle. She sank in her chair, her gaze far away. A fog of numbness surrounded her as she tried to bring her world into focus. She closed her eyes and began massaging her temples. The heavy weight of her emotions was causing a migraine to settle in. She let out a long shaky breath. In less than forty-eight hours, her world had turned upside down, and she knew it was going to take some time before she was able to turn it back. "Get it together," she whispered, the same words she used to tell herself on a daily basis after Julie left. "Just get it together," she repeated as the police scanners began loudly squawking.

"Someone's threatening to jump off the dam," the person behind the assignment desk called.

"Payson," Jason yelled across the newsroom as he stepped out of his office. "That's your lead story for tonight. Get Tegan on it. I want a cut-in as soon as she gets set up. The other stations will be all over this, so tell her to sniff out an exclusive angle."

"Tegan's headed to the mayor's conference," she called back.

"Well, pull her off that, and send Patty instead. I want Tegan on the potential jumper."

Payson waved her acknowledgment as she woke her computer. The brochure of the island caught her attention as she was logging in. She paused for a moment and stared at the pamphlet. What she wouldn't give to be there right now. Away from the craziness of her job and the sting of pain gripping her heart. "Someday soon," she whispered to herself as she called Tegan.

"You okay?" Tegan said as she picked up on the first ring.

"Yeah. But change of plans. I need you at the dam ASAP. Looks like someone is threating to jump. Let me know once you get set up, we'll do a cut-in. Oh, and Jason said to work your juju and sniff out an exclusive angle."

"Who's covering the mayor?" Tegan sighed.

"I'm putting Patty on that. You're better with active situations. This will be the lead, so you'll go live at the top of the show. Text me when you get there."

"Roger that."

As the clock ticked closer to showtime, Payson felt like she was walking down the middle of a foggy road, dodging headlights speeding at her. Several times, she found herself back in the bathroom, leaning against the stall door, eyes closed as she tried to breathe in a moment of sanity. All she wanted to do was sit by herself, have a good cry, and be left alone. She had given away a part of her heart last night, and not only had it felt good, it had felt right. As though that little beating muscle intuitively knew it was united with a long-lost soul mate.

"Well," she whispered to herself. "Seems like my soul mate has already checked out and skipped town. So much for our rendezvous tonight," she said in disgust. But as another round of tears trickled down her cheek, she couldn't help but glance at the empty cubicle behind her. A phantom, a ghost, a temp, a character in costume sitting on a rooftop…a lover. Whatever Hannah truly was, she was definitely one thing. She was someone who'd awakened a part of her and had reminded her of what life—and love—was really about.

"I need to go on that vacation," she mumbled. Maybe even hook up with someone and have a romantic fling. Something to keep the flame now lit inside her glowing. Because one thing was for sure, there wasn't anything in her present life that could.

CHAPTER ELEVEN

Hannah and Piper appeared in the back of the arena where Oriana was training a young class of archers. Oriana glanced at them, then turned back to her students. "A quiver of arrows starting now. And concentrate on your form. I don't want to see anyone slouching," she demanded, then tilted her head toward a section away from eyes and ears.

"I see you not only broke the binding spell, but you picked up a stray." Oriana nodded to Tucker as they gathered.

"I promised him I'd take him away from the place that caused him pain. He will live with me if he so chooses." Hannah placed Tucker on the ground, then extended her arms to Oriana, palms up. Oriana placed her arms on top and leaned forward until their foreheads touched. Hannah closed her eyes and let out a contented breath. She was home.

"You look well. Glowing, I would almost say," Oriana said as she pulled out of the greeting

Hannah lowered her head. "Oriana, I—"

"I know," Oriana scoffed. "You interfered with the magic and denied the two their fate. Their star, for now, will remain dark. And all because you felt the need to bed her?" She arched an accusatory brow. Hannah remained silent as Oriana took a moment and paced. "Hannah, what were you thinking? What has gotten into you?"

"I…um…they just weren't right for each other," she said in a low voice. "I know you think I failed in my mission, but I'm telling you, I saw it. The chemistry wasn't there. Payson even assured me that she wants to be with me, but more than that…" Hannah placed a hand over her heart. "I felt the truth in here."

"Are you saying Danika made a mistake?" Oriana smirked as if warning Hannah that she was skating on thin ice.

"I, um…I meant no disrespect. Danika is a master at her craft and revered by many. Myself included." She paused, knowing her next words would be almost blasphemy. "But maybe, this one time, she may have misread the stars. So, yes, I do believe in my heart that she was wrong." If Danika really had read the night sky accurately, then why had Payson chosen her over Madison?

Oriana's pacing increased. "You thought she was wrong? You know nothing of the stars," she snapped. "Of how the night sky speaks to Danika and about her interpretations. You are a cupid, not a reader of the universe. If the night sky said they should be together, you had no right to interfere. You of all of us know better, and yet you still chose to defy the very foundation of what makes you, and all the other cupids, who you are."

But Hannah felt like she wasn't defying who she was. If anything, she was humbly opening herself up to the fairy tale that she so openly mocked. One she had refused to believe because it meant an unknown magic existed that not only rivaled her arrows but seemed to be more mystical than any spell. "Oriana, there are tales about love at first sight. Maybe in this case, those tales are more than folklore. Because the moment I laid eyes on her, I was hit with a magic all its own. It was so powerful and alluring. I have never felt such a pull. Such an absolute desire to be with someone."

"Do not mistake a lustful impulse for love. You are not meant to be together, Hannah. Have I not taught you better than this?"

She stared at Oriana. "You're wrong, we *are* meant to be together. Every instinct inside me says so." Hannah closed the distance between them. "Have you not also taught me to listen to the truth in my gut? To assess a situation for what it is instead of how it's perceived? To believe with your heart in—"

"Enough!" Oriana snapped with a wave of her hand. "I will not have my words thrown back at me to justify a tryst. What you did was wrong, and unfortunately, we have no magic to correct your indiscretion. For now, the spell between the marks will remain broken. Let us hope the universe grants them a second chance at a star." Oriana glared at her. "A star that will not have your name on it. Do you understand?"

A rebuttal was on the tip of Hannah's tongue, but she knew better than to utter a single syllable. Instead, she lowered her head and conceded the argument but not her feelings. What she did might have been wrong in the eyes of the island, but it was the right thing for her heart. She would find her own way around this dilemma. "I understand."

"Good. Then we shall never speak of this again. I will inform Dafina that you are no longer feeling ill and will be returning to your duties immediately. As for this conversation and the events that took place, I never want to hear another word of it again. Am I making myself clear?" She glared at Hannah and Piper.

They nodded.

"Good, then we're done here," Oriana took a step away, then paused. "She's a mortal, Hannah," she said over her shoulder. "You may think you know her, but you don't." She ran the back of her hand over her scar. "They are not to be trusted, especially with your heart. I will not lose my best archer to a misplaced emotion of desire. We may play a role in their love lives, but they do not and should not ever play a role in ours. It might have been wrong for me to have sent you there. Maybe some mistakes should be left unfixed," she muttered and returned to her students.

Hannah took a step in Oriana's direction as another statement to defend her actions formed on her lips but paused when Piper squeezed her forearm. "Don't," Piper said in a low voice. "Now's not the time or place."

Hannah glanced at Piper's hand, then at Oriana. She wanted to storm over and tell her how wrong she was to so promptly dismiss her feelings. This was not a tryst or anything like her past experiences with the island women. This called upon the emotions she had heard so many speak about when they'd experienced love.

She scooped up Tucker and let Piper lead her out of the courtyard.

"Well," Piper said in a lighthearted way. "That was intense. I don't think I've ever seen Oriana so—"

"I'm going to challenge the law," Hannah said as defiance burned through her. No one was going to tell her who she should and shouldn't love. To deny her the happiness they themselves had found. No, this was something she wasn't going to walk away from. This was something worth fighting for.

"Which law?"

"The one that says no mortals are allowed on the island. I'd like to ask Payson to live with me."

Piper stopped walking and turned to her. "Were you not listening to anything Oriana said? Leave it alone, Hannah. If you pursue this, nothing good will come of it. Look…" Piper placed a hand on her shoulder and softened her tone. "You're back where you belong, no one will ever know the truth of what happened, and you're free to woo as many island ladies as you desire. In fact, whaddaya say we head over to Brea's this evening for a little fun?"

Hannah shrugged out of her grip. She didn't want to go to Brea's tonight, and she definitely didn't want to hook up with anyone. All she wanted to do was hold Payson in her arms and make love to her. "Not tonight. I, um, I've already made plans."

Piper slowly circled her like a drill sergeant. "You're going back to see her, aren't you?"

For the first time in their friendship, Hannah felt like lying to Piper. She was tired of feeling like a scolded child. Why couldn't Piper take her side and sympathize with her? To understand her love for Payson was the very thing they'd dedicated their lives to. But instead, she avoided Piper's stare as she nodded.

Piper scoffed in her face. "Leave her be, Hannah. You're back among your true family. What could you possibly gain by keeping that liaison alive?"

"She's more than that."

"Really?" Piper smirked. "How is this one any different from the rest?"

"It's different because *I'm* different. For the first time, I actually want to get to know someone. To create a life with them."

"Are you listening to yourself? Really hearing what you're saying? Hannah, the heavens presented *their* names, not yours."

"Well, they're wrong."

"So you keep saying. Look, what you're alluding to is ludicrous and flies in the face of all that we are. You're saying that the magic I spent my entire life mastering and the countless arrows I crafted on Danika's orders were all flawed? Think about what that says."

"I don't think they were all flawed. It's just that, in this particular case, I believe there was a misread."

"Oh, so you're saying the process, in all the other cases throughout history, has worked but now, because you became enamored with a mark, you're questioning everything we stand for."

"I am not questioning what we stand for. It's just…" She trailed off as she turned to Piper. "If you could feel what I feel, you would know. When she touches me, I tingle in a way I've never felt. When we're apart, I count the moments until I see her again, and when we're together, I never want to let her go. I don't know how else to describe it. It's like a sudden addiction that I can't satisfy."

"I'm not denying your feelings. I saw enough to know your interaction would end in delight, but how many times have I heard you talk about other women giving you that same pleasure?"

"It's not the same. With Payson, it's different."

"Different enough to jeopardize all that you have? Look around at your life and tell me if fighting for a mortal is really worth losing all this." Piper extended her arm and gestured to the land. "She can't live here, Hannah, and let's be honest, do you really think you could live among the mortals? What would you do? And how soon would you start resenting everything you gave up for her?"

"Maybe, since she can't come here, I can split my time and be with her every evening after I've finished my cupid duties."

"And what kind of life would that be? You would not be around for Bella or for evening gatherings at Brea's. And how about your archery skills? You're constantly training with Oriana, and even though you complain about it, I know you love your time with her. How are you going to do that while living a mortal life?"

Hannah remained silent. She loved everything about her life. And never once had she considered questioning any part of it. Oriana was right, being a cupid was in her blood; it was a part of her. That she had no doubt about. But there was something else that was also a part of her: Payson. She had never known her heart was missing a piece of itself until last night. But could she really live the life Piper described? Her heart pounded a resounding yes, but her mind said no. She lowered her head and hunched her shoulders as she began questioning her decision. Tears fell like a light sprinkle of raindrops around her feet as Piper pulled her into a hug.

"Let her go. Her name will appear again in the sky, linked to another. She will find her true love." Piper broke the hug. "And eventually, so will you."

Hannah nodded as she wiped the wetness from her cheek. Why did this have to be so complicated? To have to make a decision between the love for another or the love for all she had ever known seemed cruel and unjust.

"Now, come on, let's get you home."

"I think for now,"—Hannah glanced at Piper—"if you don't mind, I just want to be alone."

"I understand. But please don't wallow in this for too long. Put it out of your mind. You're home where you belong. You'll see. It won't take long before you're back into the swing of things."

"Perhaps."

"So I'll see you tonight at Brea's?"

She gave Piper a half-hearted smile as she again wiped her cheeks, and they parted company. Would she soon be back into the swing? No, not even close. Although it was true that she was glad to be home, without Payson by her side, she feared she would eventually feel unsettled here. She kicked the ground as she walked. If she was surer of her and Payson's fate, surer that the universe gave its blessing, she would fight for overturning the law instead of doubting what she'd done. If she really did choose Payson, they might make it for a little while, but without a star in the night sky that sealed their fate, they were—according to island belief—destined to fail.

An hour later, Hannah entered her house, quickly changed, and was grateful to finally be rid of the mortal clothing. "Stay here, sweetie, there's somewhere I need to go." She bent and kissed Tucker on the head. He jumped on her couch and curled into a ball. She stepped on the porch and blew three short whistles. A minute later, Bella trotted up, and Hannah buried her face in her neck. "I've missed you so." Bella whinnied. "Whaddaya say we go for a little ride?" Bella bobbed her head as Hannah gracefully threw herself over her back. "To the lake, my friend."

She entwined her fingers in the thick mane as Bella reared and took off in a full canter. Hannah arched her back, tightened her thighs, and tilted her face to the sun. Oriana was right about one thing. The island was the breath of her life, and she loved it with the very essence of her soul.

Ten minutes later, she dismounted, stripped her clothes off, and jumped into the lake. The water was warm and soothing as she backstroked away from the shore. She treaded water for a few minutes as she soaked in the beauty around her. No tall buildings, no neon signs, no police scanner squawking in the background. Just nature in all its splendor, surrounding and singing to her. *This* was what life was about.

She turned on her back and floated, her face and breasts sticking out of the water. All sound was muffled, and the buoyancy of the water gave her the sensation that she was hovering on a cloud of air. And even though her body was in a complete state of stillness and calm, her mind was moving a mile a minute. Were her feelings for Payson just lust, as Piper had suggested?

No, her heart whispered back. This was more than a simple hormonal reaction. She thought about the elderly couple at the casino restaurant. The expression in the man's eyes as he caringly fed his wife and the way she looked at him in return. *That* was the look of love, and *that* was what she held in her heart for Payson.

She wanted what that couple had. She wanted to grow old with the woman she loved and wake every morning to see her beautiful face and give her the softest of kisses. She let out a shaky breath as she thought about living her life with the mortals. She could sell her golden arrows in exchange for their currency and buy a place somewhere she and Payson both could live. A parcel of land that wasn't walled-in with buildings and concrete. And if the currency ran out, she'd figure out a way to make more.

On the other hand, the list of things she would miss about her life on the island seemed endless. "This is insane," she said as she slowly swam back to shore. She was second-guessing everything without even knowing if Payson wanted to be with her. Or even if she would consider living on the island. And if she did, that would be the fuel she would use to petition Nikita about the law. And if Nikita refused, *then* she would make a decision. "No sense thinking about leaving until I have to," she mused to herself. *First thing's first…*she needed to talk to Payson about their future plans and get a feel for what she wanted.

She finished the last few strokes with a renewed sense of energy. She shook the water from her hair and took a moment to sit on the grass and let the sun dry her as a small cyclone of wind kicked up and circled her.

"Oh no, you don't." She stood and tried to shoo away the wind. "I'm mad at you. If it weren't for you blowing away my arrow, none of this would have happened. You had the power to guide that arrow into her, and instead, you…" Hannah paused as she replayed that moment in her mind: the tingle she'd gotten from looking into Payson's eyes and the realization that she'd actually *seen* Hannah. Her hesitation at the instant connection and the weird gust of wind that had blown her arrow so completely off target. What if the wind knew what she did not? That a mistake *had* been made, and Payson and she were the ones who were destined to be together.

"You knew, didn't you?" she said as she poked at the air, and the wind played the notes that confirmed her suspicion. She threw her head back in laughter as she spun in a circle and held her arms out. "You knew," she repeated as a lightness surrounded her heart. The wind stilled, and Hannah bowed. "Thank you, my friend. Thank you," she whispered as a breeze tousled her hair, then became still again.

It was the confirmation she needed to put her fears and doubts aside, and she now knew what she had to do and where her destiny lay. One way or another, she would be with the woman who'd captured her heart with as much magic as any of Piper's arrows and spells.

❖

It was late, and the newsroom had an almost eerie stillness to the air. The calm before the next storm, Payson thought as she gathered her purse. The morning news crew would be here soon, and the room would once again be filled with a flutter of activity. As she shut her computer down, she glanced at the corner office. Jason was staring at his computer, hands hovering over the keyboard. He took a quick glance in her direction, and as she waved a good night, her phone chimed.

"Hey, Tegan," she said as she pushed open the back door.

"Please tell me you're coming out tonight. I really think it'll do you some good."

Payson pinched the bridge of her nose. She was exhausted mentally and physically, and she was in no mood to socialize with anyone. Not even Tegan. All she wanted to do was go home, pour a glass of wine, and be left alone. The night that couldn't come soon enough she now just wanted to be over. "No, I just want to go home."

"Want me to come over and keep you company?"

"No, but thanks anyway. I just…" She trailed off as her breath caught in her throat, and her stomach bottomed out. "I… uh," she muttered as she focused on Hannah leaning against her car with a bouquet of flowers in hand. She was wearing her usual black jeans and white collared shirt, but she had her cuffs rolled up, exposing large golden bracelets. "I'll call you right back." She ended the call and stood staring at Hannah as goose bumps tickled her skin. A part of her wanted to run into her arms and kiss her deep, while the other part wanted to tell her off. And as she approached Hannah, that was the part that won the emotional tug of war.

"If those flowers are for me, you can keep them." She brushed past as she unlocked her car. "In fact, I'm a little shocked you're even here. I figured since you already checked out of your hotel room, you would have skipped town by now."

"What are you talking about? I told you I would be here," Hannah said.

"You told me a lot of things, Hannah Archer, or whoever you are," she said with a bite. "Look, I don't know what your game is or what you're trying to get out of me, but I'm on to you. I had Tegan do some digging into who you really are, and she said you're a ghost."

"A ghost?" Hannah snickered. "I'm not sure what Tegan meant by that, but I can assure you, I'm as alive as you are."

"It's not meant in the literal sense. It means you're someone who flies under the radar so they're not detected. It means," she spat, "you're just like my ex." Tears began to sting her eyes. She did not want to cry in front of Hannah. In fact, she didn't want to cry over this anymore.

"Payson, I swear, I can explain."

"Uh-huh, sure. Now, if you'll excuse me, I want to go home. It's been a long day." She folded into her car and shut the door. She was not in the mood for excuses. Now or ever. People that told the truth didn't have to go back and explain themselves.

"Payson, please. Will you just stop for a moment and listen to me?"

Payson heard the muffled plea, lowered the window, and white-knuckled the steering wheel. She took a breath, calmed herself, and rubbed the sweat from her palms on her jeans. "You have five minutes. Then I'm driving away, and you and I and whatever it was we started will be through."

Hannah nodded. "I'm a…" She trailed off and averted her eyes.

Payson blinked once, then twice, as she waited for Hannah to complete the sentence. But when no other words came, she rolled her eyes in irritation. "You can't even explain yourself, can you?" she muttered.

Hannah lowered her head and mumbled, "I'm not quite who I appear to be."

"Tell me something I don't already know," Payson said as she began to drive away. She was not about to be fooled twice.

"I'm a cupid," Hannah blurted, and Payson slammed on her brakes. *Wait, did she just say what I think she just said?*

Hannah approached her window. "I know what that sounds like, and I wouldn't blame you for thinking I'm crazy, but I'm telling the truth. I'm a cupid from a place called Archer Island, and I was originally sent here to get you and Madison together."

"Me and Madison?" Well, that at least explained her annoying push to get them together.

Hannah nodded. "You were destined for one another, but I, um, I kinda screwed up and missed when I was trying to shoot you with her companion arrow. So I was sent here to correct my mistake, but instead, I've since learned that you and Madison are not destined for love. You and I are."

Oh, this was not only beyond delusional, it was starting to feel a little creepy. "Okay, wait, back up…you said you're a cupid? As in a stripper?"

"What? No, Payson, I'm a cupid, as in, a matchmaker of love. I travel the world and shoot golden arrows at would-be lovers so their destiny will be sealed in the sky with a star."

Payson let out a cynical laugh. "Wow. Okay…yeah. Uh-huh. Now, *you* listen. I'm going to drive away from you and whatever imaginary place you live in, and I'm never going to look back."

"No," Hannah cried. "Payson, you have to believe me. I am willing to give up everything to be with you. Please, don't go. Have dinner with me so we can talk through this. Please, Payson…please."

Tears began flowing down her cheeks as Hannah's pleading words pierced her heart, and the pull to be with her tugged at her. The voice in her gut screamed for her to back her car up, yet her mind was already in protective mode. She needed to shield herself from any further pain that being around Hannah would cause.

Just rip the bandage off, she encouraged herself. *Drive away now, go home, and cry it off. It'll hurt less than prolonging it over a dinner laced with ridiculous stories.* She already knew everything she needed to know. "Don't ever come around me again. I don't want to see you, hear from you, or in any way be around you," she called out the window as she nodded encouragement to herself, kept her head forward, and slowly drove out of the parking lot.

❖

"Payson," Hannah's scream carried in it the magnitude of her pain. "I love you!" The words strangled her heart. Suddenly, the brake lights came on again, and the car paused for a moment. "Payson?" Hannah whispered on a hopeful breath as the car remained frozen, and for a few seconds, she thought Payson was signaling to her. Letting her know that she loved her too, and everything would be okay. But as she took a step, the lights dimmed, and the car rolled down the street.

Hannah fell to her knees, wrapped her arms around her stomach, and began rocking as tears flooded her eyes. She had been willing to challenge an island law or contemplate giving up everything to be with her, and now she was… "Gone." She choked on the word because the air in her lungs was filled with guttural sobs. Minutes ticked by unnoticed until she felt a hand rest on her shoulder, giving it a gentle squeeze. "Payson?" she whispered as she turned. She looked up through foggy eyes and tried to make out the figure standing over her.

"I'm so sorry, my friend." Piper's soft voice lingered in the air. "I figured you'd be here when you didn't show at Brea's."

Hannah opened her mouth, but nothing came out. The words she was trying to say died, too heavy to be spoken. Piper bent, helped her up, and held her in a tight embrace.

"I need." Hannah sobbed. "To go after her."

"What you need is to come home."

"I can't, don't you understand? We are destined to be together, even the wind said so."

"Enough with the destiny thing," Piper snapped. "Hannah, you were never destined to be together. She was always meant for another. What about that can't you understand?"

"No." Hannah shook her head. "How dare you say that?"

Piper cupped Hannah face. "Look at me, Hannah…look at me. What has gotten into you? Let her have the life she was intended to have," Piper said in a low voice. "To love the person she was truly meant to be with. And as much as you want it to be, that person is not you."

Hannah pushed away. "Don't speak to me about love. What do you know about love?" She stabbed a finger forward. "You know nothing of the emotion." Piper's reputation of a one and done lover far exceeded hers. And unlike Piper, Hannah actually wanted to fall in love and settle down. Piper, on the other hand, prided herself on being untamed, as though settling down with a lover would clip her wings.

"And you think sleeping with this mortal for one night makes you an expert? I may not know what it feels like to ache for another soul like in a love song, but neither, my friend, do you."

Hannah rubbed the back of her hand over her eyes. "It's true that I've never felt the power we wield until now. But I can tell you this, for the first time, I know what the magic of love feels like. And it's amazing, Piper. It's a pull so powerful, I can't even begin to describe it. It grips you, tingles you, and possesses you. It controls your thoughts and your desires, and you crave it like a drug. I've never understood the magnitude of what the universe packs in this single emotion, but I can tell you this, once you've felt it, you never want to lose it."

Piper paused for a moment as she locked eyes with her, then pushed past, and sat on the curb, head in her hands.

"Piper?" Hannah cocked her head as she slowly walked over and sat next to her. "What's wrong?"

"The moment you told me about her, I knew there was something about this one. And it scared me because I didn't want to believe that someone could capture your heart enough to possibly take you away from the island." She averted her eyes. "I didn't want to lose my best friend."

"Oh, Piper. Nothing will ever separate us." She placed a hand under Piper's chin and raised her head. "We're bonded, you and I. There isn't a single thing in this world that could tear us apart."

"And yet, as I sat waiting for you at Brea's tonight, I knew you had already made up your mind to go after her."

Hannah hugged her. They gently rocked in each other's arms. It was true; she had been toying with the decision to leave if it came to that. But she'd never stopped to think how the other side of that decision would deeply wound the loved ones in her life. She kissed Piper's forehead. "It doesn't matter now. She's gone. I told her who I was, and instead of believing me, she, um…" She choked. "She left me. But I can't really blame her. To a mortal, I'm sure my words sounded ludicrous." Her chest was tight, and her heart was in her stomach. She was a fool to have told Payson the truth, but what else was she going to say? Another lie? She had heard enough bits and pieces about Payson's ex to know how much she hated being lied to.

"You're kidding. You really told her you're a cupid?"

Hannah nodded.

Piper chuckled. "So you basically told her you are the mortals' version of a mystical and mischievous chubby little boy who's barely dressed and has tiny wings." Piper gently nudged her. "Of course she's going to look at you like you're crazy. You asked her to believe in something they see as cartoonish."

"I just thought..." Hannah trailed off, but Piper was right. Why should Payson believe her? They'd only known each other a few days, and she was asking her to suspend her beliefs and have faith. She snorted and shook her head. What a fool she was to think this would work. She could never be herself in Payson's world, and a relationship of hidden secrets was not a relationship she wanted. "I guess I didn't totally think it through from Payson's point of view. I'm such a fool." She exhaled a heavy breath and wiped away the lingering wetness still staining her cheeks. "What now?" she said as they remained on the curb, leaning against the other.

"Now we go home. Your heart needs to heal, and there are a few souls waiting for you. In our little space on this planet, you mean the world to them."

Hannah nodded. She still had Bella, Tucker, Oriana, a handful of friends, her parents, and of course, Piper. "Okay. Let's go home," she said as Piper stood and pulled her to her feet. She'd spent two unexpected days among the mortals, and in that short amount of time, she'd found something she'd never encountered on Archer Island. She'd found love. And now she had to return knowing that what she'd found, she'd also lost. Maybe Piper was right; maybe it was never meant to be. No matter how much she wished it to be otherwise, it just wasn't. And as she glanced around the parking lot one last time, she whispered a good-bye to Payson and the love they had briefly shared. It was time she returned to a life that made sense, a life she didn't have to explain. She would bury herself in her duties, mend her heart, and hope that someday, the stars would grace the sky with her name.

❖

Piper and Hannah materialized on the porch of her house. Bella whinnied from the field and came trotting over. "I'm glad to see you, my friend," she said as she gently stroked Bella's neck. Piper opened the door, and Tucker came bounding out. "Okay, okay." Hannah giggled as he rolled over and started peeing. "I'm glad to see you too."

"Someone sure missed you," Piper said.

Hannah scooped Tucker up to a face full of kisses. This was not the night she had envisioned, but it would still be a night where she was surrounded by love. As they settled on the porch steps, Hannah rubbing Tucker's belly, she glanced at Piper. "I've lost her."

"You will find another," Piper said as she joined in the petting.

Hannah tilted her chin to the night sky. The stars of all the lovers she and other cupids had successfully united looked down upon her. She searched in the blackened areas and hoped she would spot one in the shadows, waiting to be lit with her and Payson's name. Maybe in time, their paths would cross again, and by then, the outcome would be different. She still believed they were meant to be together. Maybe it was the timing that was off, not the love.

"What are you thinking about?" Piper asked as she leaned back on her elbows.

Hannah shook her head. "Oh, nothing really."

Piper nodded. "Are you going to sleep in the hammock tonight?"

"Yep," she said as she glanced again at the sky. Maybe Payson would be stargazing tonight, and if so, Hannah wanted to feel connected to her as much as possible. "You wanna crash on the couch? I'll keep the door open so we can both enjoy the fresh air."

"You saying you'll make me breakfast in the morning?"

Hannah chuckled. "Sure, I'll make you breakfast in the morning."

"Pancakes?"

"Yeah, I can do that."

"Then I guess I'll crash on your couch."

Hannah smiled. "Well, that was easy."

They fell into a comfortable silence as Tucker curled between them, and Bella put herself to bed in the adjacent stable. And as Hannah's heart ripped apart with more thoughts of Payson, one thing was certain, those around her would do their best to help put the pieces back together.

❖

Hannah was sitting in a tree at a park, waiting for her second mark to jog by. The weather was drizzly and dreary, and it perfectly represented her mood. It had been a week since Payson had driven out of her life, and the hollow feeling she'd left behind was no closer to subsiding. She'd performed her duties on autopilot, and every night, when she'd returned home, she'd curled into her hammock with Tucker and had gazed at the stars until she'd fallen into a restless sleep. She had not been to Brea's, the lake, or to Piper's, opting to be alone.

"What has become of me?" she whispered to herself as she leaned against a branch and gazed at the sky for answers. The vibration from the companion arrow snapped her back to her task at hand. She scanned the path, and about twenty yards out was her second mark, jogging toward her. Her bow was nocked and ready to go in a blink. As the runner rounded the turn, Hannah paused as she looked at his face. She was making it a point to study those whom her arrows pierced. She wanted to remember them if ever their paths crossed again. And she had begun wondering, for the first time, how her marks had met, and what their future would hold. All questions she would never have the answers to.

Now, the wind said as it danced around her. She released the arrow and handed it over to the wind. It pierced the mark perfectly. He would never know the truth of how his love was delivered to him: Hannah's marksmanship, Piper's arrows, the guiding hands of the wind, and the writing in the night sky. And he would never know that as he rounded the bend and accidently tripped over an untied shoelace, that the person who caught his fall had been pierced moments ago by a companion arrow. Hannah wished them well as she replaced the bow on her shoulder and placed her fingers on her cuff's striped inlay.

She landed in front of her house. Piper was in the hammock with Tucker, and her horse was grazing next to Bella. "Another successful day?"

"Always," Hannah said as she slowly strolled up her porch, stripped the quiver and bow from her back, and sat on a step.

"I, um, was wondering if you were up for a drink at Brea's?"

Hannah shook her head. "I'll just hang here for tonight."

Piper swung out of the hammock, sat next to her, and placed Tucker on the ground. "You've told me that every day this week."

Hannah shrugged. She was tired of thinking and tired of feeling. She was miserable and numb and didn't feel like eating, socializing, or even talking.

"How about I bring some food over? You've lost some weight."

Hannah shrugged again. "Nah, I'm not all that hungry, but thanks anyway."

"And are you ever planning on returning to Oriana's arena for practice? She said she hasn't seen you all week."

"Maybe I'll go next week." Hannah got up, placed a loving hand on Piper's shoulder, gathered her stuff, and shuffled into her house. Tucker bounced at her heels. She placed her bow and quiver on the shelf, patted them lovingly, and flopped on her couch. Tucker jumped in her lap, and she rubbed his head as she rested hers against the cushion and let her mind drift to Payson. She had been a fool to mess with the universe, and this was her punishment. She bent forward and released a breath. She had robbed the universe of their star, and in turn, it had robbed her of her heart.

CHAPTER TWELVE

"Thanks anyway, Tegan, but I'm just not hungry," Payson said as she declined the pastry.

"Sam asked about you again today. I told him you still weren't feeling well, and he said to give you his best." Tegan shoved her hand in the white bag and pulled out an oversized oatmeal raisin cookie. "You feel like joining us tonight after the show?"

"No, not tonight, you go ahead without me. I think I just want to go home. I'm not really in the mood. Maybe next week?"

Tegan crossed her arms. "I'm starting to really worry about you."

"Thanks, but I'm fine. I just need a little more time." But it wasn't time she needed; what she really needed was to see Hannah. She had played Hannah's story over and over in her head, and the absurdity of it all was a mockery. She had given Hannah a chance to explain herself, to tell her who she really was, and instead, Hannah had chosen an explanation out of a fairy tale. What was she supposed to think?

Payson had no answers, but the fact that she was still turning it over in her head made her wonder why she couldn't let it go. Why she still couldn't let *Hannah* go. They might have only shared one night, but that night etched a tune in her heart that she couldn't stop replaying. And that was why she had taken the time to call the venues in town and ask if any were showcasing cupid performers. They'd all given her the answer she already knew to be true…none were.

Tegan nodded. "Okay, I get it, but don't be making this a habit. I really miss our after-work drink time."

"Payson!" Jason's screeching voice raced across the newsroom.

She grabbed her notepad. "Don't go too far, I have a feeling that whatever's up, you'll be a part of it."

"Oh, the joy of it all," Tegan mumbled as she focused her attention on the pastry bag and searched for another treat.

Payson sluggishly headed for the corner office. She was exhausted both mentally and physically, and all she wanted to do was go to a beach somewhere far away from him and the crap of the world and just decompress.

"I'm going to keep the rest of Sam's goodies on your desk. You need to eat," Tegan called after her.

Payson raised her arm and gave a backhanded wave as she smiled. Even if she had no intention of eating, it was nice to know someone cared. "Closed or open?" Payson referenced the door as she entered his office.

"Closed," he grumbled without looking up from his computer.

"What's up?" she asked as she took a seat.

Jason rocked back in his chair and folded his arms. "You know I don't care what anyone does in their personal life as long as it doesn't affect the show."

"Jason, I—"

He held up his hand. "I don't want to hear it. What I want is my star producer to get her head back in the game. Eight mistakes in last night's show. Ten the evening before that. So whatever it is you've got going on, leave it outside this newsroom. I want a clean show tonight."

She could have fired off an explanation about how exhausted she had been, about how she desperately needed a vacation, another producer…a life. Instead, she just nodded and got up to leave. "Anything else?"

"Yeah, put Tegan on this." He held out a torn piece of paper pinched between his fingers.

Payson snatched it, glanced at it, and chuckled. Tegan was going to have fun with this one. She walked out without looking up or saying another word. As she returned to her desk, she handed the paper over. "You're going to love this one."

"A tourist got stuck in the mouth of one of the MGM lion statues after climbing in to take a selfie?" Tegan laughed. "You gotta be kidding me."

"Your first hit will be eight minutes in."

Tegan waved her acknowledgement as she walked away. "Think about going out tonight. Please."

"I'll think about it," Payson called as she sat and woke her computer. She glanced at the brochure, untacked it, and sighed. The feeling of loneliness creeped up and stomped on her heart again as she thought about the island retreat. She wanted to be there with her toes in the sand and a tropical drink in hand and forget about the ugly and bizarre for ten amazing days and just live life.

She would have loved to go to a place like that with Hannah and make love under the stars. To caress her face and explore her mouth as her tongue penetrated deep. Her fingers teasing toward Hannah's—

The loud squawk of the police scanners startled her, and she jumped.

"An OIS off Tropicana," a voice called out.

Payson grabbed her notebook and headed to the assignment desk to get more information. An Officer Involved Shooting was never good, but it did pull in viewers. She would take Tegan off the tourist stuck in the lion statue, put her on this, and lead the show with it.

Once she gathered all the information, she shuffled back and tossed her notepad on her desk. As she grabbed her cell to call Tegan, she stared at the cubicle behind her, and the strange gut feeling resurfaced. And with it came the same faraway voice that seemed to whisper Hannah's name. Yeah, so much for gut feelings, she scoffed at herself and dismissed the sensation. Yet, there was something deep down that told her there was more to that feeling than just the simple nuance of an intuitive tingle. As the scanner screeched again in the background of her mind, she robotically hit Tegan's number and walked her through what was going on as she dismissed her feelings and shifted into autopilot.

That evening, she finished up the show with only three mistakes. When everyone gathered in the studio, she was the last to shuffle in. She listened as Jason scolded and drew attention to the errors, knowing that each word was directed at her. She kept her head down and lingered as everyone filed out in front of her.

"You going out with us tonight, Payson?" a production assistant called out as he opened the back door.

"Oh, I think I'll pass tonight, but have a drink for me."

He nodded and left as she returned to the newsroom. She glanced at the corner office, and Jason was leaning back in his chair, talking on the phone in an animated way. She knew he would probably be here another hour, reanalyzing and reevaluating the show. She looked at him, then glanced again at the tropical brochure.

No, she decided. The future that he represented was not the vison she saw for herself. She wasn't sure exactly what her future looked like, but she knew it wasn't like his. She grabbed her purse and shut down her computer.

"It's time to get off the merry-go-round," she whispered to herself. Because going around in a circle wasn't the same as going forward. "I need a life," she mumbled and made a promise to start looking for another job.

As she walked out the back door and headed toward her car, she paused as a slight wind blew past, causing her to shiver. The familiar tingle pulled at her gut, as she glanced around the parking lot. "Hannah?" she said as her instincts kicked in and told her she wasn't alone. "Anyone there?" she called out as fear gripped her.

A person appeared in front of her. Startled, she jumped back.

"Sorry, Payson, I didn't mean to scare you."

Payson scanned the woman wearing tight jeans and a T-shirt, black leather biker boots, and had a stone necklace dangling halfway down her chest. "Who are you?"

"I'm Piper. Hannah's friend."

The tension Payson was holding in her shoulders dissipated as she smiled. "So you're Piper? I've heard a lot about you."

"From Hannah?"

"Hannah and Tegan both."

"It would be nice to see Tegan again. I have never met anyone who plays cards as well as she does."

"Well, she's not here. She's over at Gimbauld's, grabbing a drink. But I'm sure she'll be at the tables soon enough."

"Thank you, but Tegan is not why I'm here. Hannah told me what happened between you two. And I just wanted to tell you that she's miserable. I've known her my entire life, and I have never seen anything get her this down."

Payson pushed past Piper and opened her car door. "You can tell Hannah I don't date people who can't be honest about who they are."

"Hannah was being very honest in who she is."

Payson closed the door and lowered her window. "Oh really? When she told me she was a cupid, as in shoot an arrow in someone's heart, that wasn't totally delusional?"

"She is a cupid. In fact, she's our island's best."

Payson stared. She needed to warn Tegan that they both seemed to be attracted to crazy women. "Sure, she is," she said as she turned over the ignition. "Now, if you'll excuse me, I'm not going to waste my time on another version of a cupid story." Payson threw the car in drive, and Piper materialized next to her. "Jeez!" She slammed on the brakes. "What the hell?" A blink later, Piper was again outside. "How did you—"

"You need to open your mind and listen to me. Really listen, Payson. Because what I'm about to tell you is going to sound crazy, but I can assure you, it's the truth. Just please, hear me out, then I'll leave you be so I can go play cards."

Payson threw the car in park and folded her arms. "Fine, you have five minutes."

Piper began telling Hannah's life story, ending with the chapter that included Payson. Five minutes turned into an hour, and although Payson's mind wrapped around the story, she spun her own version. Somewhere in everything that Piper was saying were probably bits and pieces of the truth, but Payson didn't want bits and pieces; she wanted the whole deal. When Piper finished, she reached in her front pocket and handed Payson a piece of paper.

"What's this?"

"It's where Hannah will be tomorrow morning. If you believe any of what I'm telling you, then be at that location around ten. Give it some buffer time, and look around. Really look around. A tree, a rooftop, she likes to shoot from above."

"Did you say rooftop?"

Piper nodded. "She told me that the day she was on the rooftop about to shoot Madison's companion arrow in your heart, you saw her."

Payson shook her head. She was not going to be a part of this game. No matter how many times she closed her eyes and saw Hannah sitting in all her glory on that rooftop staring at her, she refused to believe it was real. It had to have been nothing more than a trick of the mind or a weird reflection of some sort. Facts, she thought as she sat staring at Piper, she needed to wrap her head around hardcore facts that made sense to her. Facts grounded her; she could turn them over in her head and make logical decisions. She had no idea what to do with the blurred lines and elaborate lies that she had just been given. She reached over, took the paper, glanced at it, then tossed it in her purse. She had no intention of going. "Piper, I don't know what to say."

"Don't say anything, just be there. If you care at all about Hannah, give her the benefit of the doubt and see for yourself. Please, just think about it."

Payson rolled her eyes. "Fine, I'll think about it."

"Thank you," Piper said. "Now, I'm off to pay a visit to Tegan. I feel like tonight could be a lucky night with the cards. Remember, be there by ten." Piper took a step back, raised her hand over her head, snapped her fingers, and vanished.

Payson looked around. "Piper? Piper?" A moment later, her cell phone chimed with a text from Tegan.

Hey, Piper just showed up. We're going to play some blackjack. You coming out?

What the hell? How was that even possible? She glanced around the parking lot one last time, then reread Tegan's message, as the palms of her hands turned clammy. Magic was something she was very familiar with because Vegas was full of shows that tricked the eyes and fooled the mind. But this…this was like nothing she had ever seen. *No*, she began typing with a shaky hand. *Enjoy your evening. I'll catch you tomorrow.*

Okay. Night.

Night.

Payson tossed her phone in her purse and let out a deep breath. Whatever was happening was starting to really freak her out. First the overwhelming gut feelings, then Madison's sudden overt attraction, Hannah confessing she was a cupid, and now Piper just up and disappearing. Seriously…what the hell was happening? She began wondering if she was having a mental break of some sort. She reached over and pinched her wrist. "Ouch," she mumbled. Well, at least that ruled out sleepwalking.

She threw her car in drive and slowly rolled out of the lot as she thought about Piper's story. Was there any truth in what she'd said about Hannah? No. Payson chuckled at the absurdity of it all. If anything, she was the unwilling participant in some sort of twisted game they were playing. But still…she'd watched Piper disappear in front of her. It was impressive, she'd give her that, but she still thought it was nothing more than a trick. At least that explanation was one she could wrap her head around.

❖

Payson yawned as she sleepily laced up her running shoes and halfheartedly stretched. She put in her earbuds and blew kisses to the picture frames of memories as she left. The slow pace she set reflected the aftereffects of a night of minimal sleep and maximum overthinking. And no matter how hard she tried to tune out Piper's words and focus on her playlist, her mind kept drifting to Hannah as she tried to figure out the riddle in the mix.

Cupids, arrows, a mystical island, and disappearing tricks. They were the ingredients for a children's book and nothing more. Something she'd believed in at a time in her life before she'd known better. At a time when a jolly man in a red suit jumping down chimneys or a rabbit hiding colorful chicken eggs seemed plausible. Before she'd grown to realize magical things only happened behind a cloak of lies. And no matter how much she wanted to believe, there was always a wizard manipulating the scene from behind the curtain.

The thought of Hannah being a mystical being who shot arrows in people was cartoonish and idiotic. What a ridiculous explanation to present, much less hide behind. But as she hit her stride and came to the fork in the road that would send her down her usual jogging path, something in her gut told her to veer left and head to the park where Piper said Hannah would be.

"This is crazy," she muttered as she stopped, turned back, then stopped again and turned back around. What was she doing? She had told Hannah she never wanted to see her again, and here she was, actually getting excited at the thought of *accidentally* running into her. As a few butterflies took flight in her stomach, she reluctantly admitted that Hannah was harder to let go of than she had hoped. And as visions of lovemaking filled her mind for the umpteenth time, her pace quickened.

Twenty minutes later, she was bent over, taking heavy breaths, and shaking out her legs in the middle of the park. For being utterly exhausted, she was surprised at how good the morning run was feeling. She grabbed her water bottle, squinted at the morning sun, and decided to take a short break and catch her breath. "What a beautiful morning," she whispered as she sat under a tree, tilted her head back, and let the breeze mix with her sweat and cool her skin.

Kids were feeding a flock of ducks in the pond, and people were walking and jogging in both directions on the path around her. She focused on one particular young couple strolling toward her. They looked like they were on an awkward first date, and it brought her back to her high school days, when she'd tripped over her feet as much as she did her words when she found herself in the company of a woman she was attracted to. If anyone needed to be shot by cupid arrows, she smiled, it would definitely be those two. Piper's story raced back into her head, and she reluctantly found herself glancing around, searching for Hannah. Nothing.

"This is stupid." This whole morning was nothing more than an exercise in lunacy. What was she expecting to see? And if Hannah was here with a bow and arrow about to shoot people, that would make her a serial killer, not a cupid. "Time to get moving," she said, more about her life and putting this all behind her than her present jogging status. She stood and took another drink as a slight degree of disappointment creeped through her. If she had seen Hannah today, would her reaction be the same as it was the other evening? Probably not, she concluded. Her anger had subsided and had been replaced with that odd pull to see her again.

Oh well, it's probably for the best, she reasoned away. But her body was sending a very clear and different signal of its own.

As she placed her earbuds back in, a glare caught her eyes, and she squinted at a nearby tree. Her breath caught when she saw Hannah sitting on a limb, wearing the same outfit she'd worn on Sam's rooftop, and Payson marveled again at how the form-fitting material hugged every bulging muscle in her body.

A blink later, and Hannah was on her feet, bow and golden arrow in hand, aiming at the young would-be lovers. Before

Payson could utter a breath, she watched with disbelief as the first arrow hit the girl dead center. "Holy shit!" Payson ran toward the couple. She couldn't provide much medical help, but she could comfort them until emergency personal arrived. The second arrow flew past her head and pierced the young man.

As Payson ran to their aid, she realized there was nothing to tend to. The couple seemed fine as they strolled past, awkwardly smiling as though neither had a care in the world. There was no blood, no arrows sticking out of their chests, no falter in their stride, and no one around her was remotely reacting. It was as though it had never happened. But it did. She'd seen it. Just like she saw Piper vanish from the parking lot. She rubbed her temples and tried to calm her racing mind. None of this was making any sense. She turned and glanced at the tree and watched Hannah focus on the couple, smile, and mouth something that looked like, "Good luck."

"That's impossible," she said as her mind tried to explain the trickery behind what she'd seen. But as she watched Hannah shrug the bow onto her shoulders, a calmness settled her anxiety, and the emotional pull resurfaced, and as she took a step in Hannah's direction, her mind and her heart sparred with one another. She'd seen things she could not explain and had heard stories she'd refused to believe. Yet, for whatever reason, part of her was opening up to the possibilities of letting Hannah back in, if only just barely.

A slight breeze blew past. Hannah's hair moved, and she tilted her head as if listening to something. A moment later, she abruptly turned in Payson's direction, and in the process, lost her balance and fell from the branch.

"Oh my God," Payson said as she rushed over and helped her up. "Are you okay?"

"Payson." Hannah reached up. "What are you doing here?"

The moment Hannah's fingers caressed her face, an unexpected jolt surged through her, jumpstarting her heart. "I, um…Piper told me you might be here today."

Hannah cocked her head. "Piper?"

"Yeah, she paid me a visit last night at the station. She tried to convince me that what you said about the whole cupid thing was real."

"I would never lie to you, Payson." Hannah took a step closer, and Payson could see her eyes searching for a sign. "I know it's hard to wrap your head around, and I understand why you would choose not to be with me. But I just want you to know that—"

Payson leaned in and kissed her, long and slow. A part of her didn't care that Hannah thought she was Cupid, Wonder Woman or whoever. This was Vegas; a lot of people made a living performing as a fairy-tale character.

"I've missed you," she said as she cupped Hannah's face.

"You have no idea," Hannah breathed in a low soft voice.

"Hannah, I don't care what you do for a living. Just don't ever lie to me."

"Payson, I—"

"Shh." Payson ran her finger gently over Hannah's lips as she searched her eyes. "I don't have a good understanding of who you are, but there's something about you that pulls at me like a magnet. It's like my heart searches for you when you're not around."

"If I told you we were destined to be together and that somewhere in the night sky, our own star is waiting to be lit, would you believe me?"

Payson chuckled. "I believe we need to take things slow and get to know each other. So why don't we just take a big step back and start over with a dinner or coffee date and see where that goes, okay?"

"Okay," Hannah said as she tucked a strand of hair behind Payson's ear.

"I need to know more about you, to see where you live, where you work, and stuff like that. And if that goes well, then we can talk about the other stuff."

Hannah nodded.

"No more lies, Hannah, or else I'm gone. I'm serious."

"But…I…" Hannah paused, then nodded. "No more lies, I get it."

"Okay, then how about we start with dinner tonight? Are you free?"

"I am." Hannah smiled. "I'll meet you in the parking lot after the show and take you out for a late-night dinner."

Payson nodded. "I'd like that." There was an innocence about Hannah that seemed undeniably real. If she was being set up, nothing in her gut was pinging right now. In fact, just the opposite. "Okay, then, I um," Payson glanced at her watch. "I need to get going, so I guess I'll just see you tonight."

Hannah smiled and took a step back. "See you tonight. And Payson, I hope there's a part of you that at least believes some of what you've been told. Magic really is all around you. It always has been." She placed her fingers on her one bracer, and in a blink, she was gone.

Payson spun in a circle. "Hannah? Hannah?" She reached out and checked for any lingering devices or wires that might have caused the vanishing illusion. "Hannah?" She glanced around a second time and noticed a teenage boy pointing his cell phone at her.

"Are you videotaping me?" Payson approached him.

The teen chuckled. "Are you kidding? You're talking to yourself and doing some weird ass shit with your mouth and tongue. So of course, I'm going to get a video of that."

"What do you mean talking to myself? I was with another woman. Didn't you see her?"

"There's no one else but you," the teen said as he turned his phone around and played the video. Payson's brows shot up, and her face scrunched as she witnessed herself kissing and tonguing the air in a rather ridiculous manner. That was impossible. Hannah was just here. She could still smell the woody scent of her skin, see the sun glisten off her eyes, and feel her muscles flex when Payson touched her.

I hope there's a part of you that believes. Hannah's words echoed in her head as she backed away. "Impossible," she mumbled as she pinched her wrist again. "Ouch." Yep, still not sleepwalking. In the time it took her to run back to her house, she knew that video would be posted, laughed at, liked, and shared. It would make her look as crazy as she felt, which was the only other explanation for all of this. As much as the realization of having a mental break scared the shit out of her, it actually seemed more plausible than the alternative.

Believe. The word whispered in her mind as she entered her house. What did she believe in anymore? "Nothing," she mumbled as she took her earbuds out and tossed them on her coffee table. She had all but lost faith that there was such a thing as a true relationship, the world seemed like it was falling apart, and magic was nothing more than an illusion. "Believe," she muttered. Oh, how she wished she could.

CHAPTER THIRTEEN

Hannah rode Bella to the modest walled castle set on a hillside overlooking the city. Several guards flanked the gates, but any real threat to Nikita had been extinguished long ago when the uprising had been squashed and the mortals had been cast off the island. These days, those left guarding the grounds were there to deescalate any intoxicated islander from storming the castle with boisterous opinions.

As Hannah rode up to the open gates, she was greeted by Sofia, a tall woman with cropped blond hair who wore leather and steel plate armor that covered her chest and shoulders. Her sword was sheathed in a scabbard hanging from her waist. The purple cloak that distinguished her as a royal knight swayed in the slight breeze, and Hannah smiled at a distant memory of them sharing each other's bodies one night under the stars.

"Sofia," Hannah said as she flashed back to a few new positions she'd learned that night and had since perfected.

"Hannah." Sofia smiled as Bella came to a rest beside her. "Haven't seen you in a while. What brings you to the castle?"

"I was wondering if I might speak to Nikita. Is she in this morning?" Her latest encounter with Payson had renewed her courage to challenge the law that stated no mortals were allowed on the island. If Payson wanted to know more about her life, then Hannah needed the option to bring her here.

"Is all well?" Sofia asked with concern.

"Yes, I just have a pressing matter I need to run by her. You know, cupid stuff."

"Ah," Sofia said in a long, drawn-out breath. "Affairs of the heart. Well…" She scrubbed her fingers through her hair and blew out a breath. "She's kinda busy right now. Can it wait until later?"

Anxiety and unease mixed in Hannah's stomach and churned. "This is a bit of a pressing matter that…" Bella pawed at the ground and let out a loud whinny. When another horse replied, Hannah glanced around and saw Oriana's mare standing by the front of the castle. "Oriana's here?"

Sofia nodded. "She's been here all morning. They're going over plans for the expansion of the academy."

"Finally. That place has been in need of an overhaul for a while. Would you mind if I wait in the greeting room until Oriana finishes? I need to speak to her as well."

"I don't see why not." Sofia shrugged. "But don't go wandering around. I know how quickly your patience wanes." She gave a knowing grin. "I'll make sure word reaches them that you're waiting."

"Thanks, Sofia, and I hope all is well between you and Luna?"

Sofia shyly smiled as she nodded. "I've never been happier. In fact, we're expecting a baby. But don't say anything. We haven't announced it yet."

"That's wonderful news, and your secret is safe with me. You're an amazing woman, and I'm very excited for you." Hannah once again thought about Sofia's masterful touch during the one and only night they'd shared together. "You deserve nothing less than true happiness."

Sofia raised a brow. "Don't we all?"

"Yes, my dear friend, yes we do." Hannah barely tapped Bella's side, and she galloped forward. At the castle doors,

Hannah dismounted and thanked Bella for the ride. Bella bobbed her head, then settled next to Oriana's mare.

Hannah straightened the bow on her back, repositioned her quiver, took a deep breath, and walked with purpose into the castle. As soon as she entered, a flood of memories cascaded over her. She saw herself as a nervous twelve-year-old, performing in an archery exhibition in the main hall. It had been the first time she'd been in the castle, and she'd heard intimidating stories of Nikita's stern side and warnings to steer clear when that side reared its head. But after the exhibition, Nikita had approached her and requested she sit at the high table in the dining hall, where she'd been treated with the utmost of kindness and respect. Since that day, Hannah had made many appearances in the castle, and each time, she was greeted with the gentle soul she had come to associate with Nikita.

She shuffled to a bench, sat, and gently placed her bow by her side while she waited. A half hour later, her leg was bouncing so much, she decided that pacing would be the better way to burn off the pent-up energy. She was about to take the most impossible shot of her life by asking Nikita to amend her own law. And this time, neither the wind nor any of her lessons would be able to aid in the outcome. This time, she was on her own.

She stood, stretched, and meandered around, admiring the paintings of past rulers and prominent residents of the island. As she stood studying the one of Nikita and Anna, the door to the room across the hall opened, startling her. Nikita and Oriana strolled out.

"Hannah?" Oriana tilted her head with concern. "What's wrong, why are you here?"

Hannah bowed. "Forgive me. I don't have an appointment. I was waiting in the greeting room so that I might have a word with you both, but I got a little impatient, so I decided to walk the halls. I hope I didn't disturb you."

"Not at all," Nikita said as she gestured for everyone to gather back into the room. "We were just taking a break."

"Hannah, has something happened?" Oriana placed her arm around Hannah as she ushered her inside.

Hannah glanced around while she gathered her thoughts. Rolls of blueprints lay around a large table, and oversized portraits hung between several open windows. The largest amongst them was Nikita and another woman standing back-to-back, faces slightly tilted toward each other, smiling. As Hannah stepped closer, she gasped. The eyes of the other woman were the same mesmerizing shade of deep emerald as Payson's, and her features were hauntingly similar. "Gemma," she whispered as the stories of Nikita's best friend surfaced in her mind.

Gemma was not only beautiful, but she and Nikita seemed as connected as Hannah and Piper, a testament to the pain she had seen on Nikita's face when speaking of her death. What a fool she was for coming here thinking she could request an amendment to a law that was put in place because the uprising took so many loved ones, especially Gemma. Who was she to request such heartache be modified to accommodate her? It was a disrespectful and selfish appeal.

"She was a cupid like you." Nikita stood beside her as she stared at the painting. "She was funny, charming, and the ladies loved her. On the day of the uprising, the rebels were armed with guns that had been smuggled onto the island. Gemma was by my side, using her bow to help defend the castle." Nikita paused as she let out a slow breath. "She jumped in front of a bullet that was meant for me. It took her hours to succumb to the mortal wound. In that time, I called upon every magician and doctor on the island to heal her, and when none could, I begged the universe to spare her." She glanced at Hannah. "She died in my arms, and Anna has told me more than once that I have never been the same."

Hannah thought of Piper as she replied in a faraway voice, "How could you be?"

"Hannah?" Oriana placed a hand on her shoulder. "Please, what's wrong? Why are you here?"

Hannah turned and remembered the times she had been cradled by this beautiful woman. The praises she'd showered on Hannah and the rare moments when she'd joined in a healthy, yet competitive archery competition. The encouragement, the understanding, the love. Oriana was more than just her master teacher; she also held the roles of a surrogate mother, mentor, and friend.

"I…" Hannah stumbled and glanced again at the painting, then at Nikita. She lowered her head as tears dripped from her chin. Mortals brought pain to this island, and even though she knew most weren't like the rebels who had instigated the uprising, she had to admit that some were. But Payson was not of that mindset. She was kind, sweet, and her soul was pure. But how could Hannah justify asking Nikita to give ground for one mortal when they'd taken so much from her? "I…" she muttered as she flicked her eyes once again toward the painting.

"Hannah, my child," Nikita said. "What pains you so?"

Hannah slowly turned her head and gazed into eyes that seemed to hold so much wisdom, warmth, and kindness. She wiped away tears that held both sadness and hope. The words she had practiced for hours, laced with confidence and persuasion, never made it past the lump forming in her throat. Instead, she slowly unbuckled her golden bracers and handed them to Oriana. If she was going to try to make it work with Payson, then she needed to be there with her. To set up a life she could share instead of one that forbade her from ever being a part of it.

Oriana took the bracers with a shocked expression. "This is about your mark, isn't it? I told you to let her go and leave this foolishness behind you. You are a cupid, Hannah, and you have forgotten your place."

"Yes, I am a cupid, now and forever. It will always be in my blood. But if I don't take this shot, I will never forgive myself. If she can't come to me, then I must go to her. Because I know in my heart that we are destined to be together."

"Don't be a fool, Hannah. Can you honestly look me in the eyes and tell me this is what you truly want? That you can walk away from all that you are?"

"I…um." She averted her eyes and let out a breath. Was this what she truly wanted? No, not even close. But she was being fueled by pure emotion at this moment and a deep belief that she and Payson were paired souls. Since she had asked Payson to have faith and believe, she must be willing to take the same leap of faith. Faith that this decision was the right one. The one that would lead to her destiny. "I can," she confirmed through a shaky breath as she opened her eyes and gazed at Oriana.

Oriana took a step closer as if to challenge her further when Nikita spoke. "What is going on? Please, enlighten me,"

Oriana turned to her. "Seems our beloved Hannah has found a lover she would like to call her own."

Nikita smiled. "Hannah, my dear, that's wonderful."

"A mortal," Oriana grumbled.

Nikita's smile faded. "Oh, I see."

"I am aware of the law, and I will not disobey. I don't want to leave, but I can find no other solution."

"And this mortal," Nikita said as she circled Hannah. "Does she know what she is asking of you? What you are about to give up for her?"

"It's not so much what I'm giving up as much as what I'm gaining. It's like there's a song in my heart that only she knows the words to. I know that sounds crazy, but right now, I just need to see where this is going." And she needed Payson to look at her and not see someone who was half insane. To do that, Hannah needed to live a life that Payson could be a part of and understand. Without well-intentioned lies or crazy-sounding truths.

"I see," Nikita repeated as she arched a brow.

"I love this island, you know I do. It's part of my soul, and it's in my blood. But I'm afraid that if I stay here, without Payson by my side, I'll never be happy." She turned to Oriana for acknowledgement and extended her hands palms up. She needed to know that Oriana understood, on some level, why she was doing this. But Oriana didn't budge. "Oriana, please."

"No, I will not be a part of this." Oriana turned to walk away but paused when Hannah spoke.

"Oriana, my teacher…my friend," Hannah choked out. "I will never forget all you have done for me. You made me see who I am, realized my potential, and made me a better archer and person than I ever could have been on my own. But more than that, you taught me to always be true to myself. To never take for granted the gifts I have been given and to remain humble in the eyes of the universe. You have always been my strength, my guidance, and my stability. Without you, I would have never found my way." Oriana's shoulders hunched. "I will send you messages through the stars, and I will always and forever be grateful that our souls strolled side by side for a moment in time."

"Nikita," Hannah said as she turned, kneeled, and laid her bow and quiver at her feet. "Please pass these on to the next promising young archer and tell her my story. Who I was on this land and my role."

Nikita nodded.

Hannah stood. "It has been a privilege to live on this island and an honor to serve you," she said shakily as she bowed before her queen, and tears fought for space in her eyes once again. With her head held down, she slowly walked away from all she had ever known. She needed to see Piper, and she wanted to ride Bella one last time to the lake and talk to her. Since horses were forbidden to be taken from the island, she needed to say good-bye and explain why she was leaving. To tell her that she cherished their time together and hoped to one day see her again.

As she continued out of the room, she could sense their eyes on her back, and she wanted to glance one last time upon the faces of those who'd given her so much, but she couldn't bear to look at them. To see the disappointment and the hurt she was sure she was causing. As she approached the door, numbness grew with each step as both pain and doubt boiled inside her. She was in love with Payson, that she was sure of. But she was not so convinced about walking away from everything she knew. Was she really doing the right thing? If so, then why did the walls feel like they were closing in on her?

"Wait," Nikita called as she stepped through the door.

She paused and took a moment to wipe her tears before she faced them.

"You have piqued my curiosity about this mortal who holds so much of your heart in her hands. Therefore, bring her to the island so that I may meet her."

"No," Oriana said as she took a step toward her. "Have you forgotten what they did to us? The pain and suffering they—"

Nikita held up a hand, stopping all further discussion. "My memory is very clear, Oriana. I understand what I am requesting and what it means." She glanced at Hannah. "Bring her."

"Here?" Hannah stumbled. "But the—"

"Law?" Nikita finished as she slowly approached with Oriana in tow. She cupped Hannah's face. "You, my dear, are the most skilled archer this island has ever seen. I know how much you love it here. How much this island means to you.

If there is a woman who has captured your interest more than this land, I am fascinated." She took the golden bracers from Oriana and motioned for Hannah to extend her arms. "You are a cupid, my dear. A giver of love," she said as she gently fastened the cuffs back on Hannah's arms. "How can one who gives so much to so many not be given a shot at her own love?" Nikita held Hannah's wrists and searched her eyes. "Bring your lover to me, and then we shall see about the law."

"Nikita," Oriana grumbled as she stepped forward. "I strongly disagree with—"

Nikita held up a hand again. "I know the pain still lives within you, Oriana, as does mine. We both have suffered a great loss. But I have spoken, and I have my reasons. Bring her," Nikita said as she nodded to Hannah.

Hannah dropped to a knee and gently cupped Nikita's hands in hers. "Thank you," she said. "Thank you," she repeated as adrenaline surged through her, and her mind raced with all the favorable outcomes that could unfold from this gesture. "I shall return." She stood, and as she exited the room, another rush of exhilaration came over her, and she jumped, slapped the top of the door frame, and let out an excited squeal. She had just been given the opportunity to bring Payson to her world and introduce her to everyone who was important to her. She was Hannah, best cupid on Archer Island, and maybe…just maybe, she could add *and lover to Payson* to that title.

"Hannah!" Oriana barked.

"Sorry about that." Hannah froze, bowed her head, and waited to be scolded.

Nikita chuckled. "My dear, I expected nothing less from you."

Hannah smiled, bolted from the castle, and ran to Bella. She wrapped her arms around her neck and let loose the emotions that had welled inside her. Bella held a piece of her heart that she didn't want to let go of, and now, maybe she wouldn't have to. The law was still the law, but the fact that Nikita had suggested she was considering reviewing it gave her hope. "Meet me at the cottage in a few minutes," she whispered in Bella's ear, took a few steps back, and touched her one cuff.

A blink later, she was standing in her old cubicle at the TV station in Las Vegas. She shuddered as she took a moment to glance around the room. The police scanner was loudly squawking in the background, workers were scampering about, and Jason was in his office on another animated phone call. The place gave her the heebie-jeebies.

"Payson," she said. "Payson."

Payson glanced over her shoulder. "Holy shit. Hannah, what are you doing here? I thought we agreed to meet after the show."

Hannah extended her arm. "Come with me."

"You know I don't have time to go out right now. I'm in the middle of stacking the newscast."

"I know you don't believe who I am, so I'm taking you to my home to see for yourself a place that is more beautiful than any brochure." She closed the gap between them. "I spoke to our queen about you, and she has requested a meeting."

"Queen?" Payson snorted. "Hannah, I don't have time for theatrics. I have a show to write, and I'm way behind as it is. Can't all this just wait until we have dinner tonight? Then you can tell me all about—"

Hannah wrapped her arms around Payson's waist.

"What are…what are you doing?" Payson squirmed a bit.

"I'm going to make a believer out of you."

"Hannah, I really don't think this is the time or—"

Hannah touched her bracer, and a blink later, they were standing in front of her cottage.

Payson spun in a circle. "Where are we? And how did you just…" Her words trailed off as Tucker came bounding out of the door wagging his tail. "Tucker?" She kneeled to a face full of puppy kisses. "I don't understand." She looked to Hannah with frightened eyes. "Seriously, Hannah." She stood. "Where are we? What just happened?"

Hannah gently rubbed a hand down Payson's back. "Don't be scared. We're on Archer Island. This is my home," she said with pride.

"But we were just in the newsroom, and I need to finish stacking the rundown. Jason's probably..." Payson began to hyperventilate. "I need to..." She bent forward and placed her hands on her knees. "I need to check in with the reporters and rewrite some of the AP stories...and make sure production knows..."

"Payson," Hannah stepped in front of her. "Listen to me... just listen to me. Take a breath, calm down, and close your eyes."

"I don't want to calm down," Payson said with bite as she stood. "I want to know what the hell is going on."

"Payson," Hannah said in a soft voice. "Please, just close your eyes and take a couple of deep breaths."

Payson glared as her eyes remained wild and searching. "I don't want to close my eyes. I want to know what is happening?"

"Payson, just please—"

"I think I'm going to throw up." She placed her hand on her chest as she began wheezing.

"Payson...Payson. Please, listen to me. Close your eyes," Hannah pleaded. "Please, just trust me."

Payson locked eyes with Hannah, and her sporadic breathing calmed a bit, and she closed her eyes.

"Okay, good," Hannah said. "Now take four deep breaths, and on your fifth, I want you to tell me what you hear."

Payson did as instructed, and on her fifth breath, she said, "I don't hear anything."

"Yes, you do," Hannah said in a soft voice. "Listen again."

Payson tilted her head from shoulder to shoulder, then let out a long, slow breath. "I hear…" She scrunched her face. "I hear birds." She smiled. "Lots of birds and horses whinnying in the distance. I hear leaves rustling in the breeze and…" She cocked her head. "Is that water?"

"Mm-hmm," Hannah softly answered. "Now, slowly open your eyes and tell me what you see? And take the time to look around."

Payson opened her eyes. "I see…green hills, a thick forest, and clear blue skies."

Hannah tucked a strand of hair behind her ear. "Do you see a place you think you could ever call home?"

"Seriously?" Payson said a bit sarcastically as she arched a brow, then pinched her wrist. "Ouch."

"Why did you just do that?"

"Because everything in my life lately indicates that I'm either sleepwalking, delusional, or having a mental breakdown. By pinching myself, I keep ruling out the sleepwalking, so it must be one of the other two."

"You really don't believe me, do you?" Hannah's shoulders dropped, and her heart sank.

"It's true that I can't explain what I've been seeing or why there's a part of me that suddenly feels at home. I don't understand any of this, and it's scaring the shit out of me, so yeah, it's hard for me to believe that I'm *not* sitting at my desk right now and having some work-related, sleep-deprived mental slip in reality. It's all just too—"

The sound of approaching hoofs made her turn.

"While you're deciding if this is all real, there's someone I want you to meet," Hannah said as Bella came trotting over. "This is Bella."

Payson stroked Bella's neck when she lowered her head. "She's beautiful. I've always wanted a horse," she said in a faraway voice.

"I know. And I can already tell that the two of you will be good friends," Hannah said. "Look, I know this is overwhelming, and there's a part of you that is looking for the trickery or that thinks you're in a delusional state. And I get that, but we really do have a queen, and we need to go see her. So for now, can you just go with it?" Hannah led her to her porch as Bella followed close behind. "Have you ridden at all?" she asked as she placed Tucker back inside the cabin.

"When I was a kid," Payson replied.

Hannah positioned Bella so Payson could use the steps to help hop on her back. "Go ahead and jump on. We'll double up."

"You're going to ride without reins?"

"Of course. I would never restrict her head like that. Besides, she understands enough to take me where I need to go. Or…close enough." Hannah helped her up, then hopped on. "Scoot close to me and hold on tight."

Hannah's breath caught as Payson wrapped her arms around her waist. She closed her eyes and said a silent prayer. Fate had not yet been sealed between them, much less in the stars, but if the warmth that surrounded her heart was any indication, there was no doubt where her destiny lay. "You, um…" She let out a breath. "You good?"

Payson rested her chin on Hannah's shoulder. "Mm-hmm."

"Bella, um…" The butterflies in Hannah's stomach took a lap. "Bella has a smooth gait, but to the novice rider, it may seem a bit challenging."

Hannah felt her squeeze a little tighter. "In that case…" She kissed the words on Hannah's ear. "I guess I'll have to hold you tight."

"You do realize how much you're turning me on right now."

"Am I? Well, maybe this dream comes with some perks."

Hannah smiled. She was so aroused that if Nikita was not expecting them, she would have had Payson on the ground, making love to her at this moment. She placed a protective arm over Payson's and held tight to Bella's mane with her other. The urge to lower Payson's hand to take care of an itch building between her legs flashed in her mind but was quickly put to rest. The queen awaited, and they really needed to deal with the matter at hand. "To the castle," she said. There would hopefully be time later to address the other pressing matter.

Bella started off in a gentle trot, then accelerated to a smooth gallop. Payson held on, and her balance never faltered. She even whooped and hollered several times, which caused Bella to pick up her gait. Fifteen minutes later, they approached the castle grounds.

"Twice in one day." Sofia smiled as Hannah approached.

"Sofia, I'd like you to meet, Payson."

Sofia's brow shot up as she cocked her head. "Well, I'd say by the look on your face, this one must be special."

"She is," Hannah said, then guided Bella to the entrance, slid off, and took Payson in her arms. "Did you enjoy the ride?"

"Very much," she answered as she stared at the castle.

Hannah reached out and entwined their fingers. "Ready?"

Payson hesitated. "Okay, let's just say all of this is real, and I really am going in there to meet a queen. What if she doesn't like me?"

"Are you kidding?" Hannah leaned in and kissed her. "You are the most amazing, kindest, beautiful woman I've ever known. She's going to love you."

She gazed at Hannah. "Keep talking like that and I'm never going to want to wake up."

Hannah laughed as she escorted her into the castle.

"Holy shit," Payson mumbled as she spun in a circle.

"Yes," Nikita said as she strolled into the room flanked by Oriana and Anna. "It is rather stunning, isn't it?"

Hannah hurried over and bowed. "Queen Nikita, Master Archer Oriana, and beautiful Anna. May I present, Payson."

Payson gasped. "I am so sorry, I didn't mean…um, I said that phrase with the utmost of admiration."

Nikita smiled as she approached. "I can already see the similarities you two share." She extended a hand. As Payson shook it, Nikita held her grasp and searched her eyes. "And I can also see you have a kind soul. I see why our beloved Hannah is so taken by you. And those eyes…I have only once seen eyes of such color that they could mesmerize with one glance. How interesting," she muttered in a faraway voice. "How interesting indeed."

A flush spread across Payson's face as she lowered her head.

Hannah took a step in Oriana's direction with the intent to introduce her to Payson, but Oriana huffed in obvious disgust, spun, and walked away. "Oriana," Hannah called as Nikita placed a hand on her forearm.

"Let her be," Nikita said. "And understand that it has been a long time since a mortal has set foot in this castle. Some wounds only heal on the surface."

"What happened to her?"

"That is her story to tell. Now then…" Nikita gestured in the opposite direction. "You're just in time for dinner. I think you'll find that our chefs are quite talented."

Hannah glanced over her shoulder at the space that had only moments ago held Oriana as Nikita escorted them into the dining hall. From time to time, she had heard whispers of a rumor about Oriana falling in love with a mortal woman who'd ended up joining the uprising. Her scar was the result of a sword fight between them when Oriana stepped in and tried to stop her, a duel that ended with Oriana disfigured and the woman she loved fatally wounded. If the rumors were true, it was no wonder Oriana felt the way she did toward mortals returning to the island.

When they approached a long table that could easily accommodate a group of fifty or more, Hannah pulled out a chair for Payson, then settled next to her.

"Payson, tell us what life is like in the place you call home," Nikita said as plates of food were placed in front of them.

They fell into a comfortable conversation, but Payson was peppered with more questions than Hannah felt comfortable with. But as Payson handled each one with grace and a smile, the feeling of awe rose within Hannah, just as it had when Payson juggled a multitude of tasks at the station. She felt proud to be by her side.

After the meal, Nikita expressed sorrow about ending the conversation but stressed that she must get back to her duties. "It was a pleasure to spend time with you, Payson."

"The pleasure was all mine," Payson said.

"Regarding the law," Nikita said. "I will make my decision and announce it in the morning. Until then, Payson has my blessing to stay on the island tonight if she chooses."

Hannah's knees buckled at the impact of the gesture. "The right words of gratitude escape me, but I can assure you that I'm grateful beyond measure."

"The expression of love is one that should never be tamped down," Nikita said as she placed an arm around Anna's waist. "Now, go enjoy what's left of the day while I address the concerns this will undoubtably cause with the island elders."

"And Oriana?" Hannah said.

"There is much you do not know. She has a right to her feelings over this, and she will have a voice in the discussion."

"I understand." Hannah bowed and hoped that Oriana and the other elders could look beyond their physical and emotional scars and embrace some form of a new beginning. But knowing the elders, and after witnessing Oriana's reaction, she was not going to cling to hope.

They departed, and Hannah took one last glance at the castle as they rode away. She wished she could be there when they met and have a say in the discussion that would determine her future. But she was not invited to participate, so her fate rested in the hands of others.

"You okay?" Payson asked. "You seem kinda quiet."

"Just thinking," Hannah said as she shook off the feeling of helplessness. If Payson's time on this island was limited, they needed to make the most of it. "There's something I want you to see. It's a place I've been going to since I was a kid, and it's very special to me. It's about a twenty-minute ride, so hold on tight." She told Bella to take them to the lake.

"What's the deal around cars? I haven't seen a single one," Payson said as they neared the water.

"The islanders decided they didn't want them. Too much land would have to be destroyed to accommodate the roads, and it would be detrimental to the wildlife. Besides, the island isn't that big. Anywhere you need to go can be easily managed on foot or by horse. Besides, most of the islanders live in town, where everything is in close proximity. There's only a few of us that chose to live on the outskirts."

"It sounds like a wonderful way to live."

"It is." She wondered again if she could ever really leave. The answer, of course, was yes, she could physically leave, but how much of her soul would remain? How much would continue to beckon her back like a luring serenade. She swallowed the taste of dread as she thought again about the law and the stories of the uprising. Chances were, nothing would change, so for now, she needed to concentrate on the moment.

Bella came to a stop, lowered her head, and began grazing as Hannah helped Payson off her back. She watched the marveled look in Payson's eyes as she glanced around. Yes, Hannah hoped, she's starting to believe. "See the rainbow in the mist at the base of the falls? I think it's magical and one of the reasons this is my favorite spot on the island."

"It's…it's…." Payson trailed off as she strolled to the water's edge. "It's just like the brochure."

"No. It's better than that brochure," Hannah said as she began stripping off her clothes.

"What are you doing?"

"Going for a swim." Hannah dove into the lake, surfaced, and treaded water. "Come on, the water's warm and feels wonderful."

"Um." Payson hesitated a moment and looked around.

"No one's around. I promise, it's just you and me."

Payson nodded and began to slowly remove her clothes.

As Hannah stared, she thought there was something sweet yet sad in the way Payson so timidly removed her clothes. As though she was uncomfortable or embarrassed by her body, which Hannah thought could rival any of the world's statues sculpted to depict the ultimate beauty of the female form. And as Payson slowly ventured into the lake, Hannah felt her nipples harden, and goose bumps appeared on her skin as the desire to make love to Payson surfaced. Although they had made an agreement to take things slow, to let Payson get to know Hannah and trust her, right now, all she wanted to do was press her body against Payson's and feel her skin on hers.

"You know," Payson said as she stood chest-deep in the water. "I really needed this break in reality."

"If Nikita gives her blessing, 'this reality,'" Hannah said as she used air quotes. "Could be yours. I could bring you here often, or maybe…" Hannah approached and stood facing her. "If you'd like, you could live here with me." She searched Payson's eyes for permission to lean in and that Payson's erect nipples were not simply an expression of being chilled.

Payson shook her head. "There's still a part of me that can't wrap my head around any of this. In so many ways, it feels like a dream because I just can't believe this is all real." She pinched her wrist.

"Will you stop doing that," Hannah playfully held her hand. "I promise you, everything about this island…including me, is very real." Hannah kissed the words down Payson's neck. "Can you feel my lips on you?"

"Mm-hmm," Payson mumbled as she tilted her head back.

"How about this?" She licked Payson's breasts. "Can you feel this?"

"Yes," Payson whispered.

"Then know that what you feel is real. That I'm real." She cupped Payson's face. "I don't know what Nikita and the elders will decide, but if they allow it, do you think you could give up your other life for this one?"

Payson lowered her head. "That was not a life."

Hannah placed her fingers under Payson's chin and raised her gaze upward as she searched her eyes. "Then think about it, okay?"

Payson pressed against Hannah and kissed her long and soft. "I will," she whispered as she took a breath.

"Mmm, do you have any idea how much I want you right now?" Hannah whispered.

"I may have an inkling." Payson playfully pinched Hannah's nipple and quickly backstroked away.

"Oh, you're in for it now." Hannah swam after her. She caught her at the base of the waterfall as the mist of cascading water engulfed them. They treaded water for a moment before

Hannah tilted her head toward the falls. "Follow me to the other side," she said over the thunderous claps of the water. "There's a small cave with a sandy beach where we can sit."

Payson nodded, and they dove under the waterfall. As they surfaced on the other side, the sound of the water was loud but not as deafening. They swam toward the small sandy beach and stopped when they could sit waist-deep in the water. Hannah loved the backside of the falls. The humid misty feel to the air, the hypnotic sound of water hitting water, and the feeling of absolute privacy. "I come here when something's on my mind that needs sorting out. It's kinda my go-to place when I need to be alone and think."

"Oh yeah?" Payson scooted closer. "And what…" She kissed Hannah's shoulder. "Are you thinking about now?"

"Right now?" Hannah moaned.

"Mm-hmm," Payson muttered as she kissed the base of Hannah's neck.

Hannah closed her eyes. Her nipples were hard and sensitive, and she shivered at the thought of Payson's mouth on them. "Do you have any idea how many times I've thought about the night we made love?" She took control, rolled on top of Payson, and pressed her body firmly against hers as the water lapped around their waists and legs.

"Mm-hmm," Payson mumbled again as Hannah licked her wet breasts.

"How many times," she said as she tickled slowly down Payson's body, "I've thought about touching your—"

Payson grabbed Hannah's hand and brought it to her mouth. She spread Hannah's fingers apart and gently kissed and sucked each one. Hannah could feel the rush of heat gather between her legs as a moan began emanating from deep within her.

Payson leaned forward. "Take me."

Those two words sent a deep chill through Hannah's body. They told her that Payson not only trusted her, she wanted her. She kissed Payson hard, letting her know that the act of lovemaking would not be slow, gentle, or drawn out. This time, they were hungry for each other. It wasn't about the lingering moments of the buildup or the approvals subtly sought with each exploration of tongue and fingers…no, this was about release. And based on the kiss and the hip movements Payson was now performing, Hannah knew it was going to be quick and fulfilling.

She grabbed Payson's wrists and firmly pulled her arms over her head. "You good with this?" she whispered.

"Uh-huh," Payson moaned.

Hannah pressed her body into Payson's and wrapped their tongues together. She released her grip from Payson's right wrist but held firm with her left as she slid to Payson's side. Payson opened her legs wider, and Hannah played for a few seconds in the slick warmth there.

Payson broke the kiss and whispered in a heavy breath. "I want to…feel you."

Hannah had two fingers inside before she finished her statement. Payson arched her back and thrust as the water splashed to the rhythm of their movements.

"Get on your knees," Payson moaned.

"What?" Hannah leaned in closer as she continued to explore deeper in Payson.

"Your knees. Get on your knees so I can go inside you. I want us to come together."

Hannah nodded as she released Payson's other wrist, pulled herself onto her knees, and straddled her. Payson didn't waste any time entering her.

"Match my pace," Hannah muttered as the water splashed around them. "Harder…faster." As she sank deeper onto

Payson's hand, she pushed with the same intensity. "Yes," she whispered. "Right there." She squeezed her thighs as the explosion hit, followed by the sensation of Payson pulsating around her fingers. "That was beautiful," she said with a heavy breath as she bent and kissed her.

She waited until she felt Payson's throbbing subside and gently pulled out, lowered herself to the side, and nestled in Payson's arms. They tucked themselves in the warmth of the water and lay silently as their breathing calmed. Hannah closed her eyes and listened to the waterfall and the distant sound of the birds singing. But the most beautiful sound she heard was Payson's heart beating beside her.

They scooted up on the beach and let the warm mist from the waterfall blanket their bodies. Hannah softly rubbed Payson's chest until she heard her breathing turn slow and shallow. She craned her neck and gently kissed the top of Payson's head. She wondered again what the chances were that Nikita and the elders would grant Payson permission to stay on the island.

"Zero to none," she whispered. But the fact that Nikita requested to meet Payson must have meant something, right? Hannah exhaled a frustrated breath. Nikita had every right to ban mortals from this land, but Payson was not like those who wanted to pillage the island's gold and take what was not theirs. Payson would never do that. Hannah knew it to be as true as life itself.

She selfishly didn't want to live a life amongst the mortals. And the fact that they would probably never be granted the gift of making their own decision about where they wanted to begin a life together made her a bit nauseous.

"Laws," she whispered to herself as she listened to the hypnotizing sound of the waterfall and yawned. "Can sure suck." She was exhausted, and as she tried to clear her mind from worrying about the things she could not control, sleep called to her. And as much as she resisted, for she wanted to remember every minute of this moment, she eventually succumbed to its serenade.

The gush of wind that blew across Hannah's face woke her. Through a groggy head, she heard the frantic notes of the wind telling her she needed to get back. They were looking for her.

She opened her eyes and blinked in the darkness. The sun had set and the dim silver light of the full moon now filled the cave.

Payson sat up. "We need to get going."

"What?" Hannah asked.

"Something woke me and I have a feeling we need to get going."

"What do you mean something woke you? As in a voice?"

"No, more like a feeling," Payson said. "I've had them all my life, but they've never been as strong as they have been these past couple of days. Like a tingle in my gut that's trying to tell me something. You know what I mean?"

"I, um…" Hannah hesitated. Payson already doubted Hannah's reality and all that she had said. There was no way Hannah was going to confess that she not only understood exactly what Payson meant, but that she had befriended and carried on conversations with the wind. "Yeah, absolutely, I get those too. I just call it something different. Anyway." Hannah waved a hand. "I do think someone's looking for us."

Payson glanced around. "Is it safe to swim back at night?"

"As safe as it is in the day. Just follow me."

They stood and held each other in a tight embrace. Hannah's heart skipped a beat as she squeezed a little tighter. She was scared that if she let go, reality would come swooping in and tear them apart. After a moment, the wind returned, and in it, Hannah felt the same urgency as before. They needed to get going.

"Come on." She raised Payson's hand to her lips and showered it with soft kisses. "We really must go. Follow me and stay close."

Payson nodded as Hannah dove under the waterfall. The moon lit the lagoon like a perfect nightlight, and Hannah set a slow pace back to shore.

"I figured I'd find you here," Piper said as she sat on her horse at the water's edge.

Hannah walked out of the lake to her. "We fell asleep behind the falls until the wind woke me and told me someone was looking for us. Is everything okay?" she asked as she grabbed her clothes and began to dress.

"Nikita is requesting your presence," Piper answered in a flat tone.

Hannah froze. "Nikita? But I thought she said she wouldn't make a decision until tomorrow."

"I know. That's why I suggest you hurry. She has requested to see you both. Now."

"Payson, we must hurry," Hannah said, but Payson was still chest-deep in the water. "Nikita wants to see us."

"I…um." Payson brought her hand up and made a circle motion with her finger. "Maybe Piper could turn around or something?"

Piper threw her head back and chuckled. "You have chosen a shy one, my friend." She glanced at Payson. "There's nothing to be bashful of. I've seen a lot of women's bodies, and they're all beautiful."

Hannah cleared her throat. "Maybe this one time you could, you know, close your eyes or turn your head?"

Piper raised a brow as if to say *seriously*? "We don't have time for games. The queen is waiting."

"Please."

"Fine. I'll cover my eyes. But make it quick." Piper placed a hand over her eyes.

"Keep them closed," Payson called as she hurried out of the water and over to Hannah, who was holding her clothes. "Do you know what this is about?" she asked in a low voice as Hannah helped her dress.

"No, I don't, but if my stomach's reaction is any indication, it's not good."

"She doesn't usually do this?" Payson asked.

"No. If the queen said she would have an answer for us in the morning, then that stands. For her to request another meeting with us before that time means something came up. And that's never a good sign."

"Let's go, ladies, we can talk on the way," Piper announced with impatience in her voice.

"Hey," Payson glanced over. "You opened your eyes."

"You were taking too long," Piper said with a wink. "Now let's go."

As they rode to the castle, Hannah called to Piper, "I have a bad feeling about this."

Piper nodded. "I know, it isn't like Nikita to call a late-night meeting. But hey, let's hope for the best, okay?"

Fifteen minutes later, Hannah's stomach was a mix of dread and hope as they dismounted in front of the castle. She glanced at Piper, who remained on her horse. "Aren't you coming in?"

"I'm afraid this is where I leave you. The request was for you and Payson. I'm just the messenger. However, I'll wait here for you if you'd like."

Hannah desperately wanted to ask Piper to come in with them and be by her side. Piper was like a sister, and for as long as Hannah could remember, they'd conquered the ups and downs of everything life threw at them, together. They'd picked each other up when one faltered, and they did their best to always cover each other's backs. And now, as Hannah stood on shaky legs, about to be handed her fate, she wanted Piper to stand beside her because if Nikita refused to alter the law, the decision would impact Piper as much as Hannah.

But instead, she nodded and replied, "Yeah. That'd be great." She'd gotten into this predicament by herself, so it was only right she face the consequences by herself.

"Then I'll see you soon for what I hope will be a celebration."

Hannah nodded as bile burned the back of her throat, and she swallowed the impulse to vomit. Sweat began beading on her forehead as she reached for Payson's hand.

"I'm nervous." Payson entwined their fingers.

"Don't be. Everything's going to be all right," Hannah said, even though her own nerves were beating on her stomach like a punching bag. "No matter what her decision is…" She presented a forced smile. "I promise that we'll figure it out."

"Hannah, my dear," Nikita said as she approached. "Please." She gestured with a wave. "Join us in the sitting room." They followed in Nikita's wake until they settled on plush velvet chairs on the balcony of the second-story room. Three untouched glasses of wine graced a nearby table; a fourth rested in Anna's hand.

Nikita bent and kissed Anna. "I'm assuming Hannah has given you a little tour of the island?" she asked as she handed over two wineglasses.

"We just came from the lake. It's magnificent." Payson gazed at Hannah and smiled as her face blushed.

"Ah, yes…yes, it is. And on a full moon, I'm sure it's all that much more spectacular." Nikita gave them a knowing glance.

Hannah averted her eyes as she took a drink and repositioned herself in her seat. The small talk was nice, even a little distracting, but Hannah's nerves could only handle so much. She wished Nikita would get to the reason why she'd summoned them. *Just rip the bandage off and give me the bad news, then leave me alone to sort out my life.*

"I suppose you're wondering why I called for you this evening?" Nikita said as she crossed her legs and settled deep into her chair.

"I must admit, you've piqued my interest," Hannah said as she let out a shaky breath.

Nikita began fidgeting with her ring. "You have put me in an awkward place, Hannah. A place I had no intention of revisiting, as you can imagine."

Hannah nodded. "Please forgive me. That was not my—"

Nikita raised her hand. "Has Hannah filled you in on the reasons why mortals are not allowed on the island, Payson?"

Payson shook her head. "She didn't, but Piper did."

"Then you can understand why the request to have one back on this land could cause quite a flutter with the elders, for they're the ones who lost the most in the uprising."

Hannah's stomach soured with each word. She didn't mean to cause anyone trouble or for past pain to resurface. She just wanted Payson to be by her side on the most beautiful place in the world.

Nikita continued to play with her ring as she regarded Payson. "My child, you are lovely. Truly lovely. You remind me of a best friend I once had, and I can also tell that you make our Hannah happy."

Hannah was waiting for the *but. But I'm sorry, we still cannot allow mortals on the island. But no matter how lovely you are, you will never be one of us.*

"That's why it pained me to make my decision regarding Hannah's request, but I had no choice."

Hannah hung her head as she felt the words suffocate her. Tears began to drip one after the other on her lap, and as Payson reached over and squeezed her hand, she struggled to breathe. Nikita had handed the decision of whether she would stay on the island back to her to make.

"And then," Nikita continued. "Something nagged at me. Something I couldn't shake from my mind." Nikita stared at Payson again. "Your eyes, they haunted me the moment I saw you walk into the castle. The color is one of a kind, and it's unmistakable, so I asked our historian to confirm my suspicions as much as she could. You see, my dearest Gemma had a twin sister. One who chose to live with her mortal husband after the uprising. Our books show they had a daughter, and that's as far as we know."

"My mother had eyes like mine, and so did my grandma and great grandma," Payson said.

Hannah stared at Payson as the jolt of those words settled in. *That's why you could see me when I was performing my duties. You are one of us.* "Nikita, that means–"

Nikita held up her hand, silencing Hannah as she continued to address Payson. "If you are who I think you are, then the island's blood runs in you. But the elders could not confirm this because we do not trace mortal lineage, so I have no verification of what I believe in my heart to be true." She turned to Hannah. "And because of that, I'm sorry to say the final vote was not in your favor. But then my sweet Anna reminded me, rather insistently, I might add." She pulled Anna's hand to her lips and gave it a gentle kiss. "Of the day I too had to make a heartbreaking decision out of love. You see, the day I cast all mortals from Archer Island and swore to the heavens above that I would never again allow one to live on this land, I broke my own law."

"I don't understand," Hannah choked out as she wiped her cheeks.

"My love," Nikita said as she kissed Anna's hand again. "Would you like to take it from here?"

Anna nodded. "My full name is Annabella Rosa Santos, and I was born in South America."

Hannah sat upright as she stared. "Wait, you were born in South America?"

"Yes. I was three when my dad died, and my mother decided to migrate to the island. She had heard stories of its wonderful way of life. But it was hard to get here, and my mother had to make a lot of sacrifices. We finally made the journey when I was ten. My mom was a seamstress, and we settled into a small dwelling in the middle of town. When I was a teenager, she encouraged me to become a seamstress as well, but I had always been drawn to horses, so instead, I became a stable hand, tending the royal herd. I had a gift when it came to handling and riding them, so eventually, I was asked to help Princess Nikita with her equestrian skills. It wasn't long before we became lovers." Anna let the back of her hand trickle down Nikita's face as she outlined her jaw.

"We were inseparable," Nikita chimed in. "My heart beat only for her. When I became queen, we wed. Everything was wonderful, the island was in harmony, the mortals that did live here integrated and became one with the land. But when the uprising happened, I was so hurt from their betrayal and enraged at the death of Gemma that I banned all islanders not born of this land. The elders came to me that night and said by my own decree, I must cast Anna off the island. I forbade it, of course, and told them that no one shall speak of her heritage again."

Hannah stood. "So you were born a—"

"Mortal. Yes."

Nikita came up behind Hannah and placed a hand on her shoulder. "So you see, my dear, I too understand what it's like to have the hands of a mortal pull your heartstrings."

"But I don't understand. If Anna was born a mortal, how has she survived centuries on this land?"

"She shares my blood," Nikita said as she and Anna opened their hands and presented matching scars that ran the length of their palms. "Had it not been for my blood mixing with hers, we would have said our good-byes a long time ago. And life without my love by my side was a thought I couldn't bear. And that is why, after much further discussion with my wife, and away from the influence of the elders, I have decided to grant Payson permission to reside here for as long as she wishes."

Hannah dropped to her knees and placed her hands over Nikita's as she began sobbing. "Thank you," she repeated over and over as she rocked back and forth. "Thank you."

"Thank my lovely Anna. For sometimes, she reminds me of the things I have forgotten or as she puts it…are too stubborn to admit."

Hannah scooted over to her. "Thank you, Anna."

"I see so much of what we once were in you two," Anna said.

"And now," Nikita said. "We shall leave you to have the rest of the night to yourselves. I shall speak to the elders in the morning. I expect some will be accepting, while others won't. But maybe it's finally time the laws are dusted off and reviewed. Some have been around for so long, even I have forgotten why my family put them in place. And more importantly, are they still relevant?" Nikita said as she and Anna escorted them to the door. "Whether you choose to live here or not is your decision to make." Nikita gazed at Payson. "But know that you are always welcome."

"Thank you," Payson said as she bowed her head.

Hannah wrapped an arm around Payson's waist and walked out into the night sky. Piper was leaning against the wall, waiting. She turned with questioning eyes toward Hannah, who smiled and nodded. "Yes!"

Piper ran to Hannah and jumped into her arms. "I'm so happy for you."

Hannah laughed as she spun Piper in a circle, then returned her to the ground. "Thanks, Piper. Now come…" Hannah tilted her head in the direction of the town. "Join us at Brea's for a late-night drink and celebration. I thought I'd introduce Payson to what real beer tastes like."

"I would love to, but I think I'll go find Tegan for a night of card playing. Enjoy and again, I am so happy for you. Welcome to our island, Payson."

Payson approached Piper and hugged her. "Thank you for everything. And when you see Tegan, please explain as best as possible where I am and tell her that if she sees me sitting at my desk in a comatose state, do not disturb me."

"I will." Piper leaned out of the hug and stepped back.

"Piper, your necklace…it's glowing." Hannah pointed in disbelief. "How is that even possible since Payson and Madison never sealed the binding spell?"

"Well, what do you know?" She smiled as she glanced at them. "I had it recalibrated to glow if your star ever lit in the sky. Looks like it just did. Congratulations."

Hannah looked up as a bright flash appeared, then calmed into a bluish-white glimmer, and she knew in her heart that it was their star. The one that held her and Payson's names and sealed their destiny. "I knew it," she said as she looked into the eyes that had captured her heart.

"Yeah, you did," Piper said as she placed a hand on Hannah's shoulder and gave it a soft squeeze. "I'm sorry I ever doubted it," she said as she took a step back. "Do you forgive me?"

"There's nothing to forgive," Hannah said.

Piper smiled and nodded. "So, um…maybe I'll catch up with you two lovebirds later. For now, though, Lady Luck is waiting for me. See ya around." She snapped her fingers and disappeared.

Payson startled. "I don't think I'll ever get used to her just popping in and out like that."

"Yeah, she can be a bit of an exhibitionist." Hannah linked her fingers with Payson's as they turned and strolled in the direction of the city. "So you like it here, huh?"

Payson nestled against her. "I do. In fact, I never want to wake up."

As they headed toward Brea's, Hannah glanced at the twinkling names of love scattered across the night sky. She closed her eyes and said a silent thank-you to the universe for all she had been given in her life. When she opened her eyes, she leaned over and gave Payson a kiss on the cheek.

There were no arrows in the making of their love or special spells conjured up to bind them. The folklore of love at first sight proved true, and although Hannah didn't completely understand how it worked, she hoped that, going forward, the laws of attraction and the ancient ways of the cupids could work together, hand in hand. After all, she was Hannah, giver of love, and for the first time, she finally understood the true magic behind that simple word that gave so much to so many.

EPILOGUE

Hannah was riding Bella in a full gallop, as she nocked two arrows, one on top of the other. She zeroed in on her marks as she squeezed her thigh muscles tighter around Bella's ribs. She leveled her bow and steadied her hand as she stilled her mind and waited for the whisper of the wind.

Now. The notes in the breeze tickled her ear as they blew past. She released the string with a smile, and a second later, she heard applause. Bella came to a stop in front of Tegan and Piper, who were locked in a passionate kiss.

Hannah jumped off Bella and landed next to Payson, who wrapped her arms around Hannah's waist.

"Such a beautiful entrance, my love." Payson nibbled the words on her neck.

"That's Hannah, always a flare for the dramatic," Piper added as she leaned out of her kiss.

A bark by Hannah's feet sent her scooping up Tucker, who showered her with slobbery kisses. It had been a year since Payson had moved to the island, and in that time, Nikita had relaxed the law ever so slightly. She was still convinced that mortals would take advantage of the land and its resources and therefore should not be completely trusted. But for the mortals whose names were bonded in the night sky with an islander's, she granted the option of living on the land.

From time to time, Payson and Hannah had returned to Vegas to visit Tegan and check in on Sam. Piper would frequently join them, and it wasn't long before Piper and Tegan were interested in more than just getting together to play cards.

"Well, we're off to Brea's for the wedding festivities," Piper said. "Brea's transformed half her place into a gambling hall for the celebration."

"We'll be right behind you. But first, Payson and I are going to swing by the lake."

Piper frowned. "Okay, but don't be too long."

"We won't, I promise," Hannah called as she watched them head toward town, remembering the day Piper had come to her cottage looking ghost white.

"Piper, what's wrong?" she'd asked as Piper had handed her a piece of parchment. It was Danika's last read of the night sky before Nikita had insisted she retire and let her understudy take over.

Hannah had carefully opened the parchment and there, written in perfect calligraphy, were Piper's and Tegan's names. Hannah had grabbed her best friend and twirled her in a congratulatory embrace. "I'm so happy for you, Piper," she'd said. "Now you'll finally understand the true power of your arrows."

"Ready my love?" Payson's soft voice brought her back to the moment.

"Ready." Hannah held out her hand, palm up, and as Payson placed hers on top, their matching scars fitted perfectly together. They still weren't totally sure if Payson had island blood in her, so just to be safe, Hannah had donated some of hers.

"Don't forget." Payson whistled, and an older black and white tobiano paint mare came trotting over. "We have to meet with Sam and Amanda in the morning to discuss the upcoming grand opening for their new store."

Shortly after Payson had moved to the island, Hannah had sold a couple of her golden arrows and used the money to pay off Payson's credit card debt. She invested the leftover cash in the expansion of Sam and Amanda's bakery. They now had a kiosk located in one of the major casinos off the strip, a thriving online business, three stores centrally located around the city, and a fourth set to open in two weeks.

"I remembered, my love," Hannah said with a smile as Payson swung herself effortlessly onto the back of the horse known around the island as Freckles, whose human companion had transitioned over a decade ago. One day, when Payson had been walking back from town, Freckles had trotted up next to her and hadn't left her side since.

As they approached the lake, Hannah noticed Oriana sitting on her horse on the other side. She nodded to them. She had not completely embraced the amendment in the law, and it wasn't until last month, when Brea had a bit too much to drink and Hannah kept pressing her, that she confirmed the rumors about Oriana were true. "Give her time," Brea had told her. "You are still and always will be her pride and joy. She just needs to work a few things out."

Hannah glanced at Payson and smiled. She understood what it meant to give someone time to *work a few things out*, especially when dealing with their long-held beliefs.

She tilted her head up, and although she could not see the stars through the blue sky, she knew hers and Payson's was twinkling bright. She bowed her head and thanked nature, the universe, and especially, the wind. For without their guidance, and a little bit of trickery, she would've never met her perfect match.

About the Author

Toni Logan grew up in the Midwest, but soon transplanted to the land of lizards and saguaro cactus. She enjoys sunset hikes, traveling, and spending time with family and friends.

Books Available from Bold Strokes Books

Cherry on Top by Georgia Beers. A chance meeting leaves Cherry and Ellis longing for a different life, but when Ellis's search for truth crashes into Cherry's insta-filter world, do they have any hope at all of a happily ever after? (978-1-63679-158-6)

Love and Other Rare Birds by Angie Williams. Ornithologist Dr. Jamie Martin and park ranger Rowan Fleming are searching the Alaskan wilderness for a bird thought to be extinct and they're about to discover opposites really do attract. (978-1-63679-108-1)

Parallel Paradise by Mayapee Chowdhury. When their love affair is put to the test by the homophobia of their family, community, and culture, Bindi and Rimli will need to fight for a chance at love. (978-1-63679-204-0)

Perfectly Matched by Toni Logan. A beautiful Cupid named Hannah, a runaway arrow, and just seventy-two hours to fix a mishap that could be the best mistake she has ever made. (978-1-63679-120-3)

Royal Exposé by Jenny Frame. When they're grouped together for a class assignment, Poppy's enthusiasm for life and love may just save Casey's soul, but will she ever forgive Casey for using her to expose royal secrets? (978-1-63679-165-4)

Slow Burn by Missouri Vaun. A wounded wildland firefighter from California and a struggling artist find solace and love in a small southern town. (978-1-63679-098-5)

The Artist by Sheri Lewis Wohl. Detective Casey Wilson and reclusive artist Tula Crane are drawn together in a web of passion, intrigue, and art that might just hold the key to stopping a killer. (978-1-63679-150-0)

The Inconvenient Heiress by Jane Walsh. An unlikely heiress and a spinster evade the Marriage Mart only to discover true love together. (978-1-63679-173-9)

A Champion for Tinker Creek by D.C. Robeline. Lyle James has rescued his dad's auto repair business, but when city hall condemns his neighborhood, Lyle learns only trusting will save his life and help him find love. (978-1-63679-213-2)

Closed-Door Policy by Erin Zak. Going back to college is never easy, but Caroline Stevens is prepared to work hard and change her life for the better. What she's not prepared for is Dr. Atlanta Morris, her gorgeous new professor. (978-1-63679-181-4)

Homeworld by Gun Brooke. Headed by Captain Holly Crowe, the spaceship Velocity's crew journeys toward their alien ancestors' homeworld, and what they find is completely unexpected—and they're not safe. (978-1-63679-177-7)

Outland by Kristin Keppler & Allisa Bahney. Danielle Clark and Katelyn Turner can't seem to stay away from one another even as the war for the wastelands tests their loyalty to each other and to their people. (978-1-63679-154-8)

Secret Sanctuary by Nance Sparks. US Deputy Marshal Alex Trenton specializes in protecting those awaiting trial, but when danger threatens the woman she's falling for, Alex is in for the fight of her life. (978-1-63679-148-7)

Stranded Hearts by Kris Bryant, Amanda Radley, Emily Smith. In these novellas from award winning authors, fate intervenes on behalf of love when characters are unexpectedly stuck together. With too much time and an irresistible attraction, anything could happen. (978-1-63679-182-1)

The Last Lavender Sister by Melissa Brayden. Aster Lavender sells her gourmet doughnuts and keeps a low profile; she never plans on the town's temporary veterinarian swooping in and making her feel like anything but a wallflower. (978-1-63679-130-2)

The Probability of Love by Dena Blake. As Blair and Rachel keep ending up in the same place despite the odds, can a one-night stand turn into forever? Or will the bet Blair never intended to make ruin their happily ever after? (978-1-63679-188-3)

Worth a Fortune by Sam Ledel. After placing a want ad for a personal secretary, a New York heiress is surprised when the woman who got away is the one interested in the position. (978-1-63679-175-3)

A Fox in Shadow by Jane Fletcher. Cassie's mission is to add new territory to the Kavillian empire—murder, betrayal, war, and the clash of cultures ensue. (978-1-63679-142-5)

Embracing the Moon by Jeannie Levig. Just as Gwen and Taylor are exploring the new love they've found, the present and past collide, threatening the future they long to share. (978-1-63555-462-5)

Forever Comes in Threes by D. Jackson Leigh. Efficiency expert Perry Chandler's ordered life is upended when she inherits three busy terriers, and the woman she's referred to for help turns out to be her bitter podcast rival, the very sexy Dr. Ming Lee. (978-1-63679-169-2)

Heckin' Lewd: Trans and Nonbinary Erotica by Mx. Nillin Lore. If you want smutty, fearless, gender diverse erotica written by affirming own-voices folks who get it, then this is the book you've been looking for! (978-1-63679-240-8)

Missed Conception by Joy Argento. Maggie Walsh wants a relationship with Cassidy, the daughter she's only just discovered she has due to an in vitro mix-up. Heat kindles between Maggie and Cassidy's mother in a way neither expects. (978-1-63679-146-3)

Private Equity by Elle Spencer. Cassidy Bennett spends an unexpected evening at a lesbian nightclub with her notoriously reserved and demanding boss, Julia. After seeing a different side of Julia, Cassidy can't seem to shake her desire to know more. (978-1-63679-180-7)

Racing the Dawn by Sandra Barrett. After narrowly escaping a house fire, vampire Jade Murphy is unexpectedly intrigued by gorgeous firefighter Beth Jenssen, and her undead existence might just be perking up a bit. (978-1-63679-271-2)

Reclaiming Love by Amanda Radley. Sarah's tiny white lie means somehow convincing Pippa to pretend to be her girlfriend. Only the more time they spend faking it, the more real it feels. (978-1-63679-144-9)

Sol Cycle by Kimberly Cooper Griffin. An encounter in a park brings Ang and Krista together, but when Ang's attempts to help Krista go spectacularly wrong, their passion for each other might not be enough. (978-1-63679-137-1)

Trial and Error by Carsen Taite. Attorney Franco Rossi and Judge Nina Aguilar's reunion is fraught with courtroom conflict, undeniable chemistry, and danger. (978-1-63555-863-0)

A Long Way to Fall by Elle Spencer. A ski lodge, two strong-willed women, and a family feud that brings them together, but will it also tear them apart? (978-1-63679-005-3)

Barnabas Bopwright Saves the City by J. Marshall Freeman. When he uncovers a terror plot to destroy the city he loves, 15-year-old Barnabas Bopwright realizes it's up to him to save his home and bring deadly secrets into the light before it's too late. (978-1-63679-152-4)

Forever by Kris Bryant. When Savannah Edwards is invited to be the next bachelorette on the dating show When Sparks Fly, she'll show the world that finding true love on television can happen. (978-1-63679-029-9)

Ice on Wheels by Aurora Rey. All's fair in love and roller derby. That's Riley Fauchet's motto, until a new job lands her at the same company—and on the same team—as her rival Brooke Landry, the frosty jammer for the Big Easy Bruisers. (978-1-63679-179-1)

Inherit the Lightning by Bud Gundy. Darcy O'Brien and his sisters learn they are about to inherit an immense fortune, but a family mystery about to unravel after seventy years threatens to destroy everything. (978-1-63679-199-9)

Perfect Rivalry by Radclyffe. Two women set out to win the same career-making goal, but it's love that may turn out to be the final prize. (978-1-63679-216-3)

Something to Talk About by Ronica Black. Can quiet ranch owner Corey Durand give up her peaceful life and allow her feisty new neighbor into her heart? Or will past loss, present suitors, and town gossip ruin a long-awaited chance at love? (978-1-63679-114-2)

With a Minor in Murder by Karis Walsh. In the world of academia, police officer Clare Sawyer and professor Libby Hart team up to solve a murder. (978-1-63679-186-9)

Writer's Block by Ali Vali. Wyatt and Hayley might be made for each other if only they can get through nosy neighbors, the historic society, at-odds future plans, and all the secrets hidden in Wyatt's walls. (978-1-63679-021-3)

Cold Blood by Genevieve McCluer. Maybe together, Kalila and Dorenia have a chance of taking down the vampires who have eluded them all these years. And maybe, in each other, they can find a love worth living for. (978-1-63679-195-1)

Greener Pastures by Aurora Rey. When city girl and CPA Audrey Adams finds herself tending her aunt's farm, will Rowan Marshall—the charming cider maker next door—turn out to be her saving grace or the bane of her existence? (978-1-63679-116-6)

Grounded by Amanda Radley. For a second chance, Olivia and Emily will need to accept their mistakes, learn to communicate properly, and with a little help from five-year-old Henry, fall madly in love all over again. Sequel to Flight SQA016. (978-1-63679-241-5)

Journey's End by Amanda Radley. In this heartwarming conclusion to the Flight series, Olivia and Emily must finally decide what they want, what they need, and how to follow the dreams of their hearts. (978-1-63679-233-0)

Pursued: Lillian's Story by Felice Picano. Fleeing a disastrous marriage to the Lord Exchequer of England, Lillian of Ravenglass reveals an incident-filled, often bizarre, tale of great wealth and power, perfidy, and betrayal. (978-1-63679-197-5)

Secret Agent by Michelle Larkin. CIA agent Peyton North embarks on a global chase to apprehend rogue agent Zoey Blackwood, but her commitment to the mission is tested as the sparks between them ignite and their sizzling attraction approaches a point of no return. (978-1-63555-753-4)

Something Between Us by Krystina Rivers. A decade after her heart was broken under Don't Ask, Don't Tell, Kirby runs into her first love and has to decide if what's still between them is enough to heal her broken heart. (978-1-63679-135-7)

Sugar Girl by Emma L McGeown. Having traded in traditional romance for the perks of Sugar Dating, Ciara Reilly not only enjoys the no-strings-attached arrangement, she's also a hit with her clients. That is until she meets the beautiful entrepreneur Charlie Keller who makes her want to go sugar-free. (978-1-63679-156-2)

The Business of Pleasure by Ronica Black. Editor in chief Valerie Raffield is quickly becoming smitten by Lennox, the graphic artist she's hired to work remotely. But when Lennox doesn't show for their first face-to-face meeting, Valerie's heart and her business may be in jeopardy. (978-1-63679-134-0)

The Hummingbird Sanctuary by Erin Zak. The Hummingbird Sanctuary, Colorado's hottest resort destination: Come for the mountains, stay for the charm, and enjoy the drama as Olive, Eleanor, and Harriet figure out the meaning of true friendship. (978-1-63679-163-0)

The Witch Queen's Mate by Jennifer Karter. Barra and Silvi must overcome their ingrained hatred and prejudice to use Barra's magic and save both their peoples, not just from slavery, but destruction. (978-1-63679-202-6)

With a Twist by Georgia Beers. Starting over isn't easy for Amelia Martini. When the irritatingly cheerful Kirby Dupress comes into her life will Amelia be brave enough to go after the love she really wants? (978-1-63555-987-3)

BOLDSTROKESBOOKS.COM

Looking for your next great read?

Visit BOLDSTROKESBOOKS.COM
to browse our entire catalog of paperbacks, ebooks, and audiobooks.

Want the first word on what's new?
Visit our website for event info, author interviews, and blogs.

Subscribe to our free newsletter for sneak peeks, new releases, plus first notice of promos and daily bargains.

SIGN UP AT
BOLDSTROKESBOOKS.COM/signup

Bold Strokes Books
Quality and Diversity in LGBTQ Literature

Bold Strokes Books is an award-winning publisher committed to quality and diversity in LGBTQ fiction.